POPULAR GIRLS: NOTORIOUS

Popular Girls Series #1

SHEILA MICHELLE

AUTHOR'S NOTE

This 2nd edition of Popular Girls has been rewritten with a completely different storyline than the original 2015 edition, but the character names and locations are the same.

CHAPTER 1

THE RAIN CAME DOWN AT A STEADY PACE AS I WAS ON MY WAY TO my first day of school at a brand-new school. As my windshield wipers were on full speed trying their best to keep up with this torrential rain, I could barely see even with my new glasses on. I didn't know what I was more nervous about—the weather and trying to get to school, or what awaited me once I got there. I think it was more of the latter.

I finally made it. I pulled into the parking lot of Sahara Palms High School, my new school. I couldn't believe that I was here at a new school in almost the middle of the second semester. It was still surreal to me that my parents just wanted to up and move out here to Las Vegas without ever thinking how it would affect me and the little friends I had back in Wisconsin—but it was clear they didn't care. They wanted a change, said I could really use a change, and that I would thank them later on especially when I would see how beautiful the winters were here. Well, I had yet to see any beautiful weather here since it was storming like it did back home, and I didn't know how much I was going to like my new school.

I shook my umbrella as soon as I got into school and got some of the water all over a tall brunette who was wearing an expensive-looking outfit as her boyfriend had his arm around her.

"Hey, watch it! My outfit!" she angrily said to me.

"Sorry," I said as I lowered my head while her boyfriend laughed. I didn't know how this day was gonna go, but I knew that I had to try and make the best of it as my parents told me to do because I really had no choice.

I spotted the first girl's bathroom and was glad I was able to spot one so fast since I'd never been inside my new school until today. I walked towards it while the outsoles of my shoes were still soak and wet and squeaking like crazy since I was wearing my low-top Converse Chuck Taylor's in pink.

Suddenly, a fight broke out between two boys right in front of the bathroom!

I was all of the sudden right in the middle of this fight as I got pushed into the bathroom and slid right into a girl who was ready to walk out with all of her friends and I ended up knocking her to the floor!

"HEY! What the hell?!" she screamed as some of her friends helped her up.

"Sorry," I said for the second time, and hopefully I wouldn't have to say it again. A beautiful girl helped me to my feet. "Thank you."

"You're welcome," she replied with a smile.

"Who are you?" the girl who I ran into asked as she checked her expensive-looking outfit out to see if it had any marks on it, and then checked in the mirror to see if her perfectly coiffed blonde hair was still in place.

"I'm Kitty, Kitty Laine. I'm new here. Today is my first day," I replied.

The girl nodded as she sized me up. "I'm Prima, Prima Donna Queensridge. I'm a junior and so are all of my friends. What grade are you in?"

"I'm a junior, too," I replied.

The girls looked at each other as if they had some kind of visual code that they signaled to one another, and they were quite the clones. They all carried the same designer handbag—a Louis Vuitton Mono-gram Neverfull GM—one of my dream bags, but they had their initials on it with stripes of the school colors in white and light green. They looked like models—all seven of them—so I knew instantly that there wasn't a chance in hell that I'd fit in with them. They also look like they were the most popular girls in the school, which went without saying.

"Since you're new, you're invited to have lunch with us if you want. We don't want the new girl to be ignored on her first day," Prima said.

I thought she was kidding. "Are you serious?" I asked anyway.

"Absolutely, Kitty. We wanna get to know you. Can't wait. See you there," Prima said, and turned around and walked out as the other girls followed.

I continued to stare at them as they all walked out the door. I smiled as I straightened myself up in the mirror. I was invited to have lunch with the models of Sahara Palms High School. This day was turning out to be a much better day than I thought it would!

Suddenly, a girl walked out of the bathroom stall. She had on dark clothes and the same sneakers as me but in black. She came up to the sink, turned it on, and washed her hands. She dried her hands as she stared at me. "Kitty?"

"Yes?" I said. I didn't wanna ask how did she know my name because it was obvious she was in the stall while I was talking to Prima and her friends.

"I heard you talking to Prima and her friends. *Don't* have lunch with them." She abruptly left the bathroom as I stared around it in shock.

What. The. Hell.

CHAPTER 2

I COULDN'T GET MY MIND OFF OF THE MYSTERIOUS GIRL IN THE bathroom before first-period classes that told me not to have lunch with Prima and her friends today. But I already accepted the invitation so here I was, sitting at the table with Prima and her beautiful diverse group of friends, who were Ursula Steele, Prima's best friend and of mixed race; Poppy Hendrichs, who had flaming red hair, fair skin, emerald green eyes and eccentric style; Lauren Dawson, who was a gorgeous African-American girl with some of the most gorgeous curly hair I'd ever seen; Rika Nitzu, who was Asian-American and had jaw-dropping hair so long she could sit on it; Olive Lowes, a pretty brunette who seemed to be one of the more quiet ones; and Ariana Garcia, who was Hispanic-American and was just stunning with very short black hair and amazing style.

All beautiful, head-turning popular girls who seemingly ruled the school.

And now I really felt that I didn't fit in with them just on their looks and style alone, as I sat here with a graphic tee and jeans on I got from Forever 21, as well as my pink Converse Chuck Taylor sneakers and JanSport backpack. They didn't seem to be the sneaker type, but then again, I was just getting to know them so I didn't wanna prejudge, but what I did prejudge on I was right about. They were the most popular girls—called the PGs for short—in the whole school, and even the first letters in all of their names spelled out POPULAR—Prima, Olive, Poppy, Ursula, Lauren, Ariana, and Rika—and Prima said this was just by pure coincidence. I didn't know whether or not I was honored to be sitting here with them, but I knew I would soon find out.

Hopefully.

"So, Kitty, we wanna know more about you. Where are you from?" Prima asked.

"Wisconsin. Mequon, Wisconsin, to be exact," I replied.

"Meh—*what*?" Prima asked, as the rest of the PGs looked just as confused as she did.

"Mequon. It's a suburban city thirteen miles north of Milwaukee."

The PGs still looked confused.

"Okay, never heard of it," Prima said. "Well, I hope you like the fact that we chose you to be a part of our group because we run a very tight circle and haven't allowed anyone else in it except Olive here."

I looked at Olive as she nodded back to me with a smile, and then continued to sip on her green smoothie. "So, I was only chosen because I'm new?"

"Is there any other reason?" Prima asked. "If you wanna have the real All-American high-school experience, there is no other group of girls in this school or anywhere for that matter that you would wanna be with. Nothing beats being with the popular girls in this school. We're known for our status and everyone knows it. If you haven't noticed, you're getting a lot of looks just sitting here."

I looked around and Prima was right. People seemed to be amazed that I was sitting here, and I think it was mostly because I just didn't look like I fit in with them because even I didn't believe I did. I *still* couldn't get my mind off of what that girl said to me in the bathroom:

"Don't have lunch with them."

There was definitely a reason for it, and if I happened to see her again because I didn't get her name and this was a big school, then I needed to have a long talk with her because it was clear that it was something big about the PGs that had her scared to even come out of the bathroom stall while I was in there talking to them.

I looked down at my phone and saw a text:

Need to talk to you during our study period. Meet me in the library. You don't wanna miss what I have to say.

It was from Olive!

I looked at her as she stared back at me from across the table, and then her eyes switched directions as she still sipped on her smoothie.

CHAPTER 3

"GLAD YOU MET ME HERE, KITTY," OLIVE SAID, AS I SAT ACROSS from her at a table for only two people in the library. "I know you're hanging with us now, but I just couldn't say out loud in front of them what I wanna talk to you about."

"Okay," I said as my eyes were big through my glasses. I couldn't wait for what she had to tell me. "What's going on? I mean, I texted my parents this morning and told them I was hanging out with the most popular girls in the school now but didn't tell them how I met you all, and even they didn't believe me because they knew that I was anything but that at my previous school."

"Well, being a PG isn't what people think it is. In fact, we could be in some serious trouble right now and not even know it." She looked out the window that we were sitting by as if she was looking for someone.

"What is it? Are you looking for someone?"

She sighed. "No, but everyone is still looking for her." She pointed up to a flyer on a wall with a picture of a girl on it:

<u>MISSING</u>
Katerina "Kat" Black

Age: 16
Grade: 10
Student at Sahara Palms High School
Last seen at house party with friends

"Oh, my God!" I said in shock as I looked at the picture of the pretty girl who would be my age if she was found alive. "She was a student here! Oh, my God! Did you know her?"

"No, I didn't know her, but I'd seen her around here. Some of the PGs had classes with her, and said she was the biggest wannabe."

I looked confused. "Why was she a wannabe?"

"Isn't it obvious, Kitty? She was a wannabe PG."

Was?

That was interesting that she was already speaking about her in past tense.

"Were you at the house party that Kat was at?" I asked.

"No," she replied.

"Why weren't you there?"

She sighed as she lowered her head. "Because I wasn't a PG back then."

"What? I thought you were always one."

"I was let in after Olivia killed herself."

"No!" I said in a whisper in so much shock I couldn't hide it. "Why would she kill herself?"

"Because of Kat," she informed me. "She felt that the PGs were hiding what really happened to her." She leaned into me and gave me a very cold look, and it froze me into fear. "No one knows this but the PGs and now you."

"I'm listening."

She took a deep breath. "People are saying that the last people Kat was seen with were the PGs, and it was not at the house party because not only was I not there, the PGs weren't there as well, so the information on the flyer could very well be wrong. And the PGs also weren't her friends, that's the last thing they were."

I quickly covered my right hand over my mouth so I wouldn't

shriek. My eyes almost bucked out through my glasses as I looked up at the missing picture of Kat once again. "Are you serious, Olive?"

"Yes, I am. The PGs said that they absolutely weren't the last ones that Kat was seen with that night, but someone took a picture of Kat being with them, and it obviously wasn't at a house party. As you know, the PGs run a tight circle. Like I said, I was only let in because of Olivia's suicide. They wanted to keep with the group's tradition with the first letter in all of our names spelling out POPULAR, plus, they said I was just as good of a fit to be one of them as Olivia was, but they could only pick one of us."

I slapped my right palm on my forehead and shook my head. "*This is crazy,* Olive! Just what the hell have I gotten myself into already with letting Prima befriend me because it was mainly her that did. The rest of you just followed suit and agreed to it."

"I know, Kitty. I think Prima is just trying to bring some good karma her way because she knows how fucked up all of this is. I don't wanna believe any of them had anything to do with the disappearance of Kat, but why would Olivia kill herself over Kat's disappearance? I think she saw some fucked-up shit and unlike the rest of them, just couldn't live with herself."

"Were the PGs questioned in Kat's disappearance?"

"They sure were, but they were never charged with anything because even though Kat was shown in that picture with them, that didn't prove anything. Kat could've very well went off with someone else or just went off on her own after that picture was taken, or even back to the house party—no one knows for sure. Even the cops said the picture of her with the PGs didn't necessarily mean that they were the last people seen with her. Everyone at the party was saying that she was drunk and high, so who knows. But she's still missing to this day and a lot of people aren't saying it, but a lot are suspecting the PGs of having something to do with it."

"But there were other people at the party, obviously, and that picture of her with the PGs could've been taken before or after she went to that party."

"Exactly, Kitty. This is why the PGs haven't gotten in trouble for it.

They were only questioned and since I'm a PG now, my allegiance is with them and it always will be."

"But . . . but . . ." I just couldn't get out what I wanted to say.

"But, what, Kitty?"

"But if they had nothing to do with it, why did Olivia commit suicide over it?"

"That's the billion-dollar question, Kitty." She leaned into me once again. "Look, since I wasn't a PG at the time but now that I am one, I can't speak on this publicly, so I'm gonna only tell you because even though I just met you today, there's just something about you that I can trust."

"I am a very trustworthy person so you can tell me anything and rest to sure that it's safe with me."

She took another deep breath. "I'm not a hundred percent ruling them out. There is a reason why Olivia killed herself, and I just can't get the thoughts out of my head of the reasons why, and I think the main reason is that she saw something go down between Kat and the PGs and just couldn't live with what she saw, but on the other hand, the other PGs acted as if nothing happened.

"None of them could stand Kat, but she was very pretty so I think there was some jealousy there. She definitely looked like a PG, but Prima was strict about the stupid first letter in our names even though she and the others tried to convince you it was just a coincidence that all of our names spelled out POPULAR. They're full of shit, Kitty. It's no coincidence."

I grinned. "Yeah, I kinda figured that."

"But Kat definitely had what it took to be a PG and was always trying to talk to any of the PGs she had a chance to talk to about bending the rules. No one should wanna be in anyone's group that bad that they're begging everyone in the group to bend the rules and let them in. No one shouldn't wanna be popular that much because being it is not all what's cracked up to be; it feels like a damn job most of the time. It's not worth it to me."

"It isn't. It's unbelievable that Prima befriended me after I crashed into her in the bathroom this morning after I told her I was new. Thanks for helping me up off the floor; that was *so embarrassing!*"

She laughed. "You're welcome, Kitty. But please, since I told you about this and you see these flyers plastered here and trust me they're all over school on the outside and on the inside, *please* don't say anything to Prima or any of the other PGs about it because they will know that I talked to you about it and they don't like talking about it at all. It makes them mad and trust and believe, you don't wanna make any of them mad, especially Prima."

"Oh, I believe that." I looked up at the flyer again. "I did passively see them all over school, but I was so nervous about this first day that I didn't notice them like the way I should've and had no idea about the story behind them. Now that I do, I'm actually in the group that may or may not have had some involvement in it. This is nuts, Olive. Never, ever did I think my first day at this school was gonna be like this!"

"Yeah, it's crazy. This is something you can definitely tell others about, but don't tell them about the PGs potential involvement in this because no one needs to know."

"Oh, I know when to keep my mouth shut about certain things."

"So, Kitty, how was school today?" my mom asked.

"It went in a way I wasn't expecting at all," I replied as I cut my lasagna.

Dad looked at me. "What? Don't tell me you already have a boyfriend?"

"Aaron!" Mom said with a grin. She turned to me. "Do you?"

I laughed. "You two *know* you're being ridiculous!"

We all laughed.

"Well, you knew we had to ask, honey," Dad said.

"So, what unexpected way did it go in?" Mom asked.

"Well, I told you both on the way home today that I'm hanging with the most popular girls in the school, but I didn't tell you how I met them," I said.

"No, you didn't, so we're listening," Mom said.

"I was going to the bathroom and when I was just about to open the door, two guys started fighting and I got pushed into the bathroom, and since the floor was slippery I slid into Prima, who happens to be the most popular girl in the whole school. I ended up knocking her down as well as falling to the ground myself."

"Oooh! Ouch!" Dad said with a grin. "I bet it would've looked funny had it been caught on video!"

"Dad!"

"Aaron!" Mom said with a grin. "That's not nice at all to say. It's actually quite embarrassing, almost all falls are." She looked at me. "So, did you get her full name?"

"Yeah, her name is Prima Donna Queensridge. Yes, that's her real name. She told me her middle and last name at lunch which she invited me to while we were in the bathroom this morning. I was surprised she introduced herself to me after crashing into her like that, and I was even more surprised when she invited me to lunch with her friends. I just knew she was gonna cuss me out and that would've been that because her outfit was beautiful."

"Wow, baby. A popular girl inviting you to sit with her at lunch with her friends. I'm sure that made you feel good," Mom said.

"It did," I replied, but didn't wanna tell them that the good feeling started to sour and sour fast after what the girl in the bathroom told me after Prima and the rest of the PGs left out of it.

"Oh, there's something I wanna show you," Dad said, and pulled his phone out of his pocket. "Do you know anything about this?"

It was the flyer of Kat Black!

"No, I don't know anything about it," I lied. "I wasn't there last year when it happened."

"We know you obviously weren't there, Kitty, but did anyone mention it to you?" he asked.

"No," I lied once again, and was already tired of doing it. "I saw the flyers all over school and I figured that since it was almost a year old, no one was really talking about it anymore."

"Well, a co-worker of mine asked me to ask you about it since you go there now," he said.

"And who's your co-worker?" I asked.

"Gus Black, Kat Black's dad," he replied.

I felt faint. Like, seriously.

"Well, if you hear anything about the case just let me know so

I can let him know. You know it's your civic duty to report anything you hear about anything when it comes to an open case, Kitty. I know it was your first day there, so let me know and your mom if you hear anything about it. You know how people like to talk."

"But that's just it. People like to talk with no facts to back up their talk. Today was my first day there and I'm hanging with the most popular girls in the whole school, I still can't believe it and I just can't say it enough. I don't wanna lose friends I just made and especially friends like them."

"Is there a reason why you feel you may lose them this soon? You just met them today," Mom said.

Dad stared at me as he ate his salad.

"No, not at all. I'm just getting to know them. Today was my first day and I had a very good one I might say, and I got some homework as well, so may I be excused?"

"Yes, go on," Mom said. "Your dad and I will do the dishes."

"Like hell I will, Carol!" Dad said with a laugh. "I got work to do, too!"

We all laughed.

Minutes later, I was up in my room not able to do anything. I called Olive.

"Kitty, hey, what's up?"

"Hi, Olive. I hope I'm not interrupting anything."

"Not at all. I just got done with my homework so all I'm doing is looking at random YouTube videos. What's up?"

"I just had to call you and tell you that my dad works with Kat's dad!"

She shrieked! "Oh, no, Kitty! Okay, now you know you can't tell the PGs this, right?"

"Yes, I know. I just thought I could tell you since you said that you trust me so I trust you as well."

"That's great to hear that you do trust me, Kitty, because they can't know a thing about this. This has got to stay between us. My goodness! Of all places your dad ended up working at it's with Kat's dad, and Kat's dad has been really involved in her case. He's been in the media a lot talking about it and that's perfectly understandable because she was his daughter."

There went that word again—*was*.

"Well, even though Kat has disappeared, there's no proof that she's no longer alive, right?"

"Exactly right, Kitty. Even though the case is almost a year old, she could very well still be alive out there somewhere. Everyone who should've been questioned about this case has been questioned over and over. I just don't know how much more the cops can do about it."

"Has anyone been questioned in Olivia's suicide?"

She sighed. "Unfortunately not because it was just that, a suicide. Olivia left no note so there was no proof that she killed herself because of what she knew about Kat's disappearance, it's just everyone's speculations about that being the reason why she killed herself. There could've been a million other reasons, but people feel that was the main one because of the timing, plus, Olivia wasn't suicidal before Kat's disappearance is what the PGs said . . . to me. They told me they didn't tell the cops this."

"Why not?"

"Because they didn't wanna look suspicious, so they told them when asked about Olivia's suicide had she always been depressed, and they simply said yes."

"I can't believe I'm hearing this."

"Yeah, this is tough to hear, but the PGs are known for looking out for themselves first. No one else matters but them."

"Well, do I matter since I'm hanging with you all now?"

"Of course you matter, Kitty. It's just that since you're new to the group, I wouldn't say anything to piss any of them off. And like I told you earlier, I especially wouldn't bring up Kat in any way possible, especially now since your dad works with Kat's dad. They should not know that under any circumstances, okay?"

"Okay, of course. I wasn't gonna say anything." I sighed. "I'm kind of scared of the PGs now, and I just met you all today."

"There's nothing to be scared of, Kitty. We're a nice group of girls, but we get in our moods like everyone—we're no different. Just keep being the nice and sweet girl that we can already see you are and every-thing will be fine."

"I will."

But I knew now that everything was far from being fine.

Just what the hell did I get myself into already?

CHAPTER 4

My eyes were wide through my glasses as I stood idly by as Prima French-kissed a guy while standing by her locker with all of the other PGs around talking as if this was a normal, everyday thing she did with her boyfriend. But I thought the kissing was a little too sexual in the halls here at school.

My eyes shifted from Prima and her man to the huge poster on the wall of Kat. These were everywhere in the halls, big or small. The school was not gonna let anyone forget that Kat was missing, as if they had a feeling that someone at the school was involved in her disappearance, and it was probably undoubtedly the truth, especially after what Olive had told me.

"See you at the party tonight, baby," he said.

"We'll continue this there, you know it," Prima replied.

"That's set in stone, baby," he said, and then walked off with his friends.

"C'mon, Kitty, we gotta get to Gym," Prima said. "See you girls later," she said to the other PGs.

"You and your boyfriend really like to show a lot of affection towards one another, huh?" I asked her with a grin.

"Jaxson's not my boyfriend," she informed me as she returned the grin. "He's just a guy I have sex with a whole lot. No commitments on either of our parts. We've been going at it since freshman year. He's one of the most popular guys in this school if you didn't know."

"No, I didn't know for sure since I'm new here, but just looking at him and his friends I did assume that. He's gorgeous and so are his friends."

"Yeah, they are. Let me know if you want me to hook you up with any of them."

I gave her a very surprised look. "I don't think any of them will be interested in me. They were talking to all of the other PGs as if I wasn't even standing there."

"Well, you hang with us, Kitty. You have your choice of any guy you want."

I wish I could believe that, I thought. "So, there's a party tonight?" I decided to ask since she hadn't mentioned it to me yet.

"Almost every Friday and Saturday night, Kitty. And you're of course invited to come along with us if you want."

"I would love to. I just have to ask my parents."

"*Please* can I go to a party tonight with my new friends?" I begged Mom and Dad as we sat at the table eating our fast-food-Friday's dinner, McDonald's.

They looked at each other as if they were trying to figure out if they should've let me.

"Yes, it's okay that you go, Kitty. But you know what you should do and what you shouldn't do at parties, it's not like you've never been to one before," Dad said.

"I know, Dad. I don't have any urge to smoke, vape, drink, do drugs, whatever. I never have. Marijuana smells like a skunk to me. I've always hated the smell of cigarette smoke and hate looking at them littered on the ground everywhere, not to mention the way it makes a person's clothes and breath smell. I also don't have any desire to drink alcohol because I see what that does to people as well. I know what vaping can do as well so it's no better than any of the other stuff out here, and never ever have I ever thought about doing drugs. I'll be fine."

"Great, dear. We just don't want anyone to tempt you to do any of it. None of it is good for you, *none of it,*" Mom said.

"I know it isn't and I won't get tempted," I pledged. "May I be excused so I can figure out what I wanna wear for tonight?"

"Yes, go on," Mom said.

"And we wanna see what you wear before you leave," Dad said with a grin, but was serious.

CHAPTER 5

"You know my parents wanted to see what I wore before I came here?" I told Olive as I sat with her on a couch at this house party that had everything going on that I promised my parents I wouldn't do . . . and much more.

She laughed. "Our parents have something in common because mine always ask to see what I'm wearing as well, but not just to parties, for school as well."

"Wow, at least my parents only do it for parties!" I laughed. "As you see, I'm wearing here what I would wear to school. Graphic tee, jeans, and sneakers are just my thing."

"It's mine, too, even though Prima wants us all to wear more skirts and dresses and tight-ass jeans and high heels so we can show off how 'great' our bodies are."

"She hasn't told me to wear any skirts or dresses or tight jeans or high heels," I informed her.

"Consider yourself lucky, Kitty, for now, because it's probably all a matter of time before she does," she said with a grin, and then took a sip of her drink. "This has too much alcohol in it. I don't like drinks that are too strong."

Shouldn't be drinking at all, I thought. "I don't have a desire to taste alcohol at all, but the color of the drink is pretty. What kind is it?"

"Sex on the Beach," she replied.

"Speaking about sex, I assume Prima is finishing what she started with Jaxson?"

Olive laughed. "Yeah, you better believe it! She's in one of the bedrooms somewhere in this big house."

"This house is beautiful. Whose is it?"

"Brennen's, he's a junior like us. His parents are out of town for the millionth time and just leave him alone to fend for himself. They say it's business, but who knows? He's only sixteen and has a few older brothers but they don't live here and some are in college. He's the best friend of Jaxson, Prima's sex mate, as all of the other PGs call him."

I looked around at the PGs and all of them had some guy around them trying to get as lucky as Jaxson was getting with Prima.

A guy approached us. "Wanna dance?" he asked Olive.

"To this?" Olive asked with a frown.

"Something wrong with it?" he asked with a grin.

"Why don't we just talk instead."

"Come on," he pulled her up off the couch.

"See you later, Kitty," she said.

"Okay," I replied with a forced smile.

This was not the kind of time I was expecting to have at this party and once again, I felt I didn't fit in.

Minutes later, Darius, a boy who was in my American Government class, came and sat next to me with two drinks in his hands. He had pretty short curly hair and beautiful, flawless dark skin, and that was rare for me to see on any guy. He offered me one of the drinks.

"No thanks. I promised my parents I wouldn't drink," I said.

"That's cool, it's great that at least someone is listening to their parents unlike the rest of us," he replied with a grin, and put the drink on the side table. "You looked bored and lonely over here."

"That's because I am," I honestly replied.

He laughed. "Yeah, even though it seems like everyone around you is having a good time, trust me, you're better off sitting here and chilling alone like this. Keeps you out of trouble."

"If I look at it that way, you're right. I'm new at Sahara Palms and I'm hanging with the PGs, the most popular girls in the whole school, and now I'm at a party where it looks as if not everyone could've gotten in it." I looked at him. "You don't seem like the type that would attend a party like this, so why are you here?"

He laughed once again. "I normally wouldn't, but my best friend is Brennen's cousin. We would usually be at one of our houses playing video games since we're hardcore gamers, but he said that the PGs were guaranteed to be here so we couldn't miss it because of that reason alone, and he was right, you all are here. My best friend has the biggest crush on Prima and Ursula, but I would do anything to make Lauren my girl."

I smiled as I looked in his direction at Lauren as she sat between two guys who were clearly competing for her attention. "Lauren is gorgeous. I think she's one of the prettiest in the group. You look like you got some competition, but she's not impossible to get since she told me in one of the classes I have with her that she doesn't have a boyfriend. She's very nice as well."

He nodded with a smile. "I can only wish. I have no chance at getting a PG. Too many other guys want them."

"Well, you don't know if you don't try. You want me to tell her that you're interested in her?"

He laughed. "Not yet. I don't think I'm ready."

"Well, whenever you're ready, let me know. I think the two of you would look very cute together."

He smiled. "Thanks, Kitty."

"I have to go to the bathroom, excuse me," I said.

"Of course," he nodded with a smile, and took out his phone.

How rude was that? Telling me that he would do anything to make another girl his girl in front of me. I know I don't look nearly as good as the PGs, but damn that was rude as hell! I thought as I tried to find the bathroom, but I had no idea where it was.

I walked down a hall and knocked on a door that was closed.

"THERE ARE OTHER BATHROOMS IN THIS HOUSE! FUCK OFF!" a male's voice yelled through the door as a female's voice laughed in response.

Okay, damn! I thought, and continued on to find another bathroom. This house was so beautiful that I decided to go on the upper level to look for one because I knew that there were more than just a few up there.

I walked around the upper level of this home and thought Brennen was a lucky guy to call such a beautiful house his home. I decided to knock on a random door, but there was no answer. I didn't know if it was the bathroom or not since most of the doors were closed and the ones that were opened weren't one of the bathrooms, so I assumed that one of the closed doors was a bathroom. I didn't hear anything in response unlike from the one downstairs so I opened the door . . . .

And Jaxson jumped up off of *Poppy*!

"Kitty! What are you doing?" Poppy asked as she quickly put on her top as Jaxson grinned big.

What are you doing? I thought he was Prima's lover, I wanted to say. "I thought this was the bathroom. Sorry," I said, and tried to turn around and leave, but suddenly got sidetracked by a picture of Kat sitting in a beautiful silver frame on a nightstand in this room and it had to of been Brennen's room. "Sorry," I said again, and closed the door fast.

I quickly walked back downstairs and looked in the kitchen area at Prima making drinks as Ursula and Ariana sat on the laps of guys at the kitchen island counter which obviously doubled as a bar. Rika was in here as well as she talked to a guy, but they were sitting on separate stools. I walked into the kitchen and saw Olive sitting at the kitchen table as she still talked to the guy who wanted to dance with her. She smiled at me; I smiled back.

"HEY, KITTY! WANT A DRINK?" Prima yelled over to me while the Vitamix blender was going.

"No thanks, Prima," I replied with a smile. "I'll just have a Canada Dry." A guy who I had yet to formally be introduced to me threw me a cold one, and I almost didn't catch it. "Thank you."

"No problem, Kitty," he replied with a smile.

He knew my name, but I didn't know his.

Poppy entered the kitchen!

We locked eyes as she walked up to me. "Hey, Kitty. Let's go outside where the air is fresher."

She wasn't fooling me. I knew exactly what she wanted to go outside for. She put her arm around me as we went out into the backyard to where the beautiful pool was, but we walked away from everyone who was out here, and I knew why.

"Look, I'm not gonna deny what you walked in on up there, and I'm glad it was you and no one else because if it was, I don't think the outcome would've been good."

"Whose room is that?" I asked.

"Brennen's," she replied. "Him and Jaxson are best friends."

I didn't know if I wanted to mention the picture of Kat I saw on Brennen's nightstand. I decided to keep it to myself because since she was in there, I knew she saw it, too. "Well, Poppy, what you do is your business so who am I to say anything?"

She smiled. "I knew I could trust you, Kitty. Even though you're new to our school and we just met you yesterday, there's something about you that I know I can trust."

She was the second PG to find me very trustworthy, and I found this interesting.

"Well, I am a very trustworthy person," I said, as I repeated the same thing I said to Olive.

I couldn't help but to think, though, how much did the PGs really trust each other?

"Prima told me that her and Jaxson aren't serious with each other."

"Doesn't matter, Kitty. She still really likes him, but I like him, too."

"Uh, oh," I blurted out. "But Jaxson's not the only guy at our school."

"*I know*, Kitty," she stressed with a lilt of anger in her voice. "I trust you about what you saw, okay? So you know what that means."

"Yeah, I know," I said.

Just what the hell did I get myself into?

Only two days since I'd known the PGs and I felt I was in way too deep with everything, and felt I was drowning by the minute.

CHAPTER 6

I PACED BACK AND FORTH IN MY ROOM AS I TRIED TO FIGURE OUT whether or not I wanted to call Olive and tell her what I saw tonight, but I just didn't know if I should've because it would've been a violation in the trust that Poppy said she had for me, and I didn't wanna do that. But I just couldn't keep it from Olive about Kat's picture being on Brennen's nightstand, something I would've never had seen if I didn't accidentally walk into his room.

I honestly didn't know what I wanted to do.

My phone rang. I looked at it to Olive's pretty face smiling back at me.

"Hey, Olive."

"Hi, Kitty. I just wanted to know how you were since it seemed like I abandoned you at the party tonight. I'm sorry I did that. The conversation with that guy was probably one of the most boring ones I'd ever had which made the whole party boring and uneventful for me."

I wish I could say the same, I thought. "It's okay, Olive. It's clear that he really likes you. I didn't wanna get in the way of that. I talked to Darius. He's in my American Government class."

"Darius is really cute, and he has a huge crush on Lauren."

"Yeah, that's what he told me. I thought it was kind of rude at first,

24

but at least he didn't lead me on and pretended as if he was interested in me just because I sat there by myself after you'd left to talk to that guy."

"I wish I would've just stayed there and talked to you."

We laughed.

"So, did you have a good time at your very first Sahara Palms High School party?"

"I won't forget it," I replied, and that was in more ways than one.

"So, it sounds like you had a better time than I did so that's great."

I couldn't take it anymore. "Olive?"

"Yeah?"

"Is Brennen related to Kat?"

"That was his girlfriend at the time she went missing," she informed me.

I wasn't surprised. "Oh, okay."

"Who told you about the two of them?"

"Darius," I blurted out. I just couldn't mention that I had walked into Brennen's bedroom for a second to find Jaxson all on top of Poppy. I knew better.

"Oh, okay," Olive said as if it was no big deal. "Well, I better go since I'm getting tired and just wanna get some real sleep. Talk to you later."

"Okay."

Olive pressed the button to end the call. "So, how much do you trust her now?" she asked *Poppy*!

"Well, I have to say that I'm impressed so far," Poppy replied, and then got up out of the chair at Olive's desk and began pacing in her room. "I can't believe she walked in on me and Jaxson. But I'm glad it was her instead of one of the other PGs and at the very worst, Prima. I know her and Jaxson have never been boyfriend-girlfriend, but it doesn't matter, Prima has always acted as if they have been and all guys that she has an interest in is off limits, especially ones that's she's having sex with like Jaxson. He's the one that she's always going at it with."

"Well, if you like him that much, Poppy, then I think you should ask her if she's ever gonna be his real girlfriend or even ask him so you can see where the two of them really stand."

"I did ask him, and he said their relationship stands where it has always stood. He feels the two of them are never gonna be boyfriend-girlfriend at this point, and he says he really doesn't wanna be; says there's too many girls out there."

"And it sounds like he's treating the both of you as the too many girls and not a special girl to him like he should."

"I know, Olive, okay? You know you're the only one that knows about me and Jaxson because I just don't trust the others that they won't tell Prima about this, especially Ursula. I just feel that he likes me more than he likes Prima. He's just openly affectionate with her because she's Prima Donna Queensridge, *the* PG of the PGs."

"I try to look at all of us as equal," Olive said.

"So do I, but that's wishful thinking. Do you think anyone is looking at Kitty as equal since Prima let her into the group yesterday?"

"Unfortunately, I know no one is. People have been really talking about Prima letting her into the group and questioning why. It does seem like she has ulterior motives by doing what she did, even though she hasn't said anything."

Poppy sat back on Olive's desk chair. "How much have you told her about Kat?"

"Not much. I just told her about people thinking that the PGs had something to do with her disappearance, but I assured her that none of you did."

She nodded. "That's because we didn't. I don't know who she went off with that night, but it wasn't with me."

"Not me, either, especially since I wasn't with you all at the time. But remember the picture someone took of Kat talking to all of you before she went missing and there are claims that y'all were the last people seen with her."

"It's all bullshit, Olive, and you know it. I don't know why Olivia ended her life over Kat's disappearance because we had nothing to do with it. She had nothing to be guilty of just because of that picture. I wish we all knew who took that picture of all of us but we will probably never know. But Olivia's suicide is confusing to me, I can't lie."

"It's confusing to me as well; it is to all of us. But do you think Kat is still alive?"

"I honestly don't know, Olive. If she isn't, the PGs had nothing to do with it. If she is, we still have nothing to do with it. We all have our own issues to deal with, especially me now that Kitty caught me having sex with Prima's self-proclaimed man."

"But Jaxson hasn't officially claimed her and I don't believe he ever will. If what he told you is what he told you about Prima and him, Poppy, believe him."

"I wish I could a hundred percent, but a big part of me just can't."

"I understand."

CHAPTER 7

I sat at my desk during English III as I tried to pay attention on this rainy Monday morning.

Yeah, still raining.

I thought this city got more than three-hundred days of sunshine a year. I couldn't tell.

Suddenly, my phone popped up with a text even though I didn't have the volume turned up since I was in class. I looked at it and saw that it was from someone that I'd never heard of:

Hey, are you Kitty Laine?

Yes, I texted back.

You don't know me, but my name is Zoe. I'm Kat Black's sister.

I almost dropped my phone back down on my desk.

I heard you hang with the PGs now. I really need to talk to you ASAP.

I looked around as Poppy stared back at me, and then into the eyes of Mr. Lambert as he slowly took my phone out of my hand without looking at it and put it on his desk along with the seven other phones that he'd taken out of the students' hands in the class for this period. There was quiet laughter throughout the room.

I felt my face turn red in total embarrassment as I tried to now pay attention more in class knowing that our phones were always returned to us at the end of the class period.

"Thanks for meeting me here," Zoe said, as we stood in a park that was in her gated community of over a hundred nice-size homes.

"You're welcome, Zoe. I was surprised to hear from you because it seems like no one really talks about your sister. I'm new to Sahara Palms so I knew nothing about her disappearance until the first day when I was there when I saw all of the flyers of her all around the school. I haven't seen you around school."

"That's because I transferred out for my sophomore year to a private school since I was a freshman last year when this happened. I just had to talk to you since my friends that still go to Sahara Palms told me that you hang around the PGs. I just know they have something to do with my sister's disappearance, and I know they told you about her."

"No, actually, they haven't talked to me about her," I lied.

"What? You're kidding, Kitty!"

"No, I'm not," I lied again and felt very bad about doing it. "All I know is what people have said and about a picture that claimed that they were the last ones seen with her, but no one could prove it. The PGs obviously don't like talking about it because since I do hang with them, I think they would've told me about it by now."

"That's because they're guilty of her disappearance, that's why. I'm not believing otherwise." She started walking around the park and I walked beside her. "I just hated that Kat acted as if she had to be a part of their group. It was clear they didn't want her to be. I thought she was just as pretty as them, even prettier, and they seemed jealous of her because she was. But it was obviously something about her that they didn't like, and I never knew what it was and she really never knew what it was. I kept telling her time and time again that it wasn't that serious to be a part of their group, and they weren't all that just because of their popular status.

"But Kat cared about status and all of the good things that came with a popular status like the PGs. She wanted that status. She wanted that fame. She wanted that attention. She wanted to be a PG *bad*. There was really nothing I could do to convince her that she already had good friends and me—her sister and friend—but she wasn't trying to hear any of us."

"That's very unfortunate. I still don't believe the PGs had anything to do with her disappearance. What about her boyfriend Brennen?"

"He was questioned like everyone else about it and was cleared. I don't think he had anything to do with it honestly. Even though he reached out to me and my family after her disappearance and was there for us at her vigil and all, I don't believe at all that he had anything to do with her disappearance, even my family and friends don't think he did."

I didn't wanna say that I was at Brennen's house on Friday and saw the picture of Kat in a beautiful silver frame on his nightstand in his bedroom because I didn't want it to look like I was up in the room doing with Brennen what I caught Jaxson and Poppy doing. I would've just found it very disrespectful for Brennen to want to do anything with any girl since his girlfriend was still missing, and I really hoped that he wasn't.

"Listen, Kitty. I know you have the biggest connection to the PGs and have all of the inside information about how they really are, even though you've only been with them for a couple of days. Why they decided to let you in their group and denied my sister a million times it seems is something only they know, and I'm not about to ask them. They have always given me bad vibes, that's why I never wanted my sister hanging around them and was glad that they rejected her. I thought it was for her own good, but I think they got more than just tired of her. Pictures don't lie."

"Yeah, but people do," I said.

She stared at me. "Yeah, you're right, Kitty. People do. They sure do."

I knew she was trying to get me to believe that she believed that the PGs were lying about not being involved in her sister's disappearance. "I know, Zoe. Since you're her sister, I will keep you informed of course. It's just that what I tell you, you can't tell anyone that I did, okay?"

She smiled. "Okay."

We shook hands.

"Oh, and how did you get my number?"

"My dad. He told me that your dad works with him."

I nodded. "I should've known because my dad did tell me that he does work with your dad. But let's just keep the conversations we have about your sister between us unless it's something that I find out that we have to tell them about."

"It's a deal."

We shook hands once again.

"It's just that if the PGs had something to do with this, I don't want them to think they're invincible to any and everything. They act like they're all wrapped up in pink bows with gold glitter and are God's gift to this world or something, and it's not right. Like I said, I don't feel like how the rest of the world feels about them, and as you see this is in despite of what some think about them having something to do with my sister's disappearance. I believe that some people think that certain people can do no wrong, and I believe the PGs are those type that people think that about."

I nodded once again and looked at my phone at a text. "I have to go. It's my mom. She just told me that the PGs are at my house."

CHAPTER 8

I WALKED INTO MY HOUSE AND INTO THE FAMILY ROOM TO FIND THE PGs talking to my parents with bottles of Dasani water in their hands as they sat with their legs crossed on the large sofa. I looked around the room and noticed that one PG was missing.

"Hey, ladies," I said. "Where's Poppy?"

"Out to dinner with her family," Prima said with a smile.

"Oh, okay. Well, let's go on upstairs to my room," I said.

"So, where were you just before you got here?" Prima asked as she sat in my desk chair.

The PGs stared at me as they waited for me to answer.

"I was at Starbucks getting my favorite drink," I lied.

"And what drink is that?" Ariana asked.

"Caramel Frappuccino," I replied.

"That's one of my favorites," Lauren said.

"I love any of the iced teas, especially the white tea with lemonade in it," Rika said.

"That unicorn drink was great that they used to have there," Ursula said.

"Too much sugar so it was not for me," Ariana said. "But I love any of the ones with dragonfruit in them."

"I prefer anything with a little coffee flavor in it," Olive said.

"Did we come over here to talk about Starbucks drinks?" Prima asked.

They all got quiet.

Prima looked at me. "Kitty, we came over here because people have been talking about the disappearance of Kat Black. I don't know why they're bringing this up again since it's been almost a year, but I just want you to know we had nothing to do with it just in case there are people out there who want to poison your mind into believing otherwise."

I looked at Olive. She looked at me and then looked away. "No, there's no one poisoning my mind about the case. I see the posters and flyers all over the walls every day at school and was curious about her disappearance, but since you cleared it up in terms of all of your involvement in it, I don't have to ask any questions."

"Good, because there are no questions to ask," Prima said. "We had nothing to do with it and that's all we're gonna say about it. We know now that we've become notorious to people because of their thoughts of us having something to do with it, but we had nothing to do with it."

"I think Brennen had something to do with it," Ursula said.

"Why?" I blurted out.

"Because he's her boyfriend," Ursula replied.

"That didn't mean he had anything to do with it. I know they always get blamed first, but that doesn't mean he automatically had something to do with it," I said.

"Well, whatever," Prima said. "The fact is, *we* had nothing to do with it, and we just wanted that on the record that we told you since you hang with us now."

"Thank you for telling me," I said, because I didn't know when or if they were ever going to since Olive told me they didn't like to talk about it.

"So, what do you think of Prima telling me about the PGs not having anything to do with the disappearance of Kat?" I asked Olive as I talked to her on the phone later on that night.

"I'm surprised that they told you," she replied. "I really am. I just knew they would never bring it up to you. Maybe they didn't have anything to do with it, or that's what they're trying to make you and everyone else think."

"I hope it's the former," I said.

"So, were you really at Starbucks earlier?"

I paused. "No, I wasn't."

"Where were you?"

I took a deep breath. I wanted to tell her that it was none of her business because it really wasn't, but she was the one who told me about the PG's alleged involvement in this case, so I'd felt that I owed it to her to tell her. "I was talking to Zoe."

"Zoe? Zoe *Black*? Kat's sister?"

I took another deep breath. "Yes."

"It's okay, Kitty. I won't tell the other PGs. What did the two of you talk about? Well, that's a dumb question—I know why she wanted to talk to you—so, did she tell you anything new?"

"Nothing at all. It's just crazy that I'm all wrapped up in this and I haven't even been at Sahara Palms for a week."

"I know, Kitty. No one has the kind of new-girl story that you have, I bet."

"Yeah, I bet you're right!"

We laughed.

"So, was Prima telling the truth about Poppy being at dinner with her family?"

"I have no idea. That's what she told us when we all met up at your home to talk to you."

I felt a bad vibe rush through me.

"Have you talked to Poppy since being at school?"

"No, I haven't. Relax, Kitty, I'm sure she's fine."

"I know, but with everything that's going on right now, I just wanna be sure."

"Well, if you wanna be sure then call her yourself. I'll get off the phone since I have homework I haven't started yet, and if my parents find me talking on it while I'm supposed to be doing my homework then I'll have to turn my phone completely off and give it to them until I'm done."

I laughed. "That's exactly what I have to do!"

"I'm sure it's what most of us kids have to do. See you tomorrow."

"Okay."

I sat at my desk trying to figure out if I wanted to call Poppy or not. I didn't wanna seem like I was the type who was always worrying about everyone, but I knew I would not have been able to concentrate on my homework until I'd talked to her.

"Hey, Kitty! What's up?" Poppy asked.

"Hi, Poppy. I just wanted to see how you were."

"I'm just fine. Why?"

"Just wondering."

We sat in silence for a few awkward seconds.

"Hello? Kitty?"

"I'm here," I said.

"I wish I could talk more, but my mom just called me to dinner so I have to go. Talk to you tomorrow."

I hung up with my mouth hung wide open.

Prima lied to me.

She lied to me and all of the PGs were in agreement with her lying to me, including Olive. They all sat right here in my house and lied to me about where Poppy was. There was no way she was having dinner twice. Who the hell does that?

What the hell was going on and why wasn't Poppy told about coming over to my house earlier?

Something was going on and now I really had to wonder just what the hell I'd gotten myself into by agreeing to be a part of their group. This started to scare me, and I felt I had no one to really talk to about this because I just didn't trust anyone that they wouldn't go back and tell the PGs what I'd told them, but I had to talk to someone. I didn't even feel Olive was safe to talk to anymore, but she was really my only option at this point since she was a part of the group and knew them better than anyone, but in a lot of ways, she acted as if some part of her was an outsider just as much as I felt like I was, even though I wasn't.

Prima and the PGs had a lot to explain to me about Kat and now about Poppy not being invited over my house, and I was determined to find out what the hell was going on.

CHAPTER 9

I T WAS EXACTLY ONE WEEK SINCE I'D BEEN AT SAHARA PALMS HIGH School and a part of the PGs, one of the most popular high-school girl groups in the world but were known to be one of the most notorious ones as well because of Kat, so that was not good.

I talked to Olive by her locker. All of the PGs were here except for Poppy. "Where's Poppy? I thought she would've been here by now."

"She's obviously just running late since she's been here all this week," Olive said.

"That's true," I said, as Prima was all over Jaxson. I was surprised no teacher ever talked to them because I thought they were being a little too sexually explicit with each other here.

Suddenly, a girl came running out of the bathroom screaming!

"OH, MY GOD! OH, MY GOD!" she kept yelling.

And this sent everyone running to the bathroom, including me and the PGs. We ran into the bathroom with other girls and two female teachers and shrieked in shock . . . .

Poppy was lying in one of the bathroom stalls on the floor slumped over on her right side!

There was blood everywhere in the stall.

"CALL 911 NOW!" one of the teachers yelled at any of us who were in here as she checked to see if she was still alive.

I was so shocked I couldn't even move. I couldn't believe this was Poppy. I felt like I was in a nightmare as I stared at her. She wasn't moving at all.

"Kitty Laine?"

"Yes?" I said, as I wiped my eyes with a tissue since I couldn't get myself to stop crying since I'd seen Poppy laying lifeless in the bathroom stall.

"Hi, I'm Detective Jennifer Markson. How are you holding up?"

"As well as I can," I replied. "Why am I here?"

"Because you're one of Poppy's friends. We're questioning all of her friends first and foremost."

"Are the rest of the PGs here?"

"Yes, the rest of the Popular Girls are here. I've known about you all for years, my niece admires you all and follows you all on all of her social media pages. It was actually her text she'd sent to me saying that something bad had happened to one of you in the bathroom at your school. She's still in middle school, by the way."

I smiled. It was surreal to hear all of this, but it didn't surprise me. "Well, Prima just let me into the group exactly around this time last week. I'm new to the school and this is my first full week there."

"It's been a hell of a week, huh?"

"That's an understatement."

We laughed.

She opened a folder. "Well, Kitty, you've confirmed what I'm looking at here in these reports. You are a new student and hang with the PGs. Yeah, we had them in here last year because of the Kat Black disappearance. That case is still unfortunately unsolved."

"I know. This is way too much for us to have to deal with. How is Poppy?"

"She's hanging in there. The doctors said she should make it, but she has a long recovery. She's very lucky she was found when she was.

We just wanna find out if anything recent led to what'd happened to her this morning in the bathroom."

"I didn't see anything."

"That's not what I asked, Kitty," she said as she glared at me. "If there's something that led to this then you need to tell me right now because this could make the case a lot easier to solve."

I shook my head. "I have no idea who could've done this to her. Like I said and as you know, I'm new to the group. I'm still just getting to know all of the PGs. It's only been a week since I've been knowing them so you have to understand that I don't know everything about them."

"There was a party on Friday night at Brennen Conti's house, right?"

"Yeah, there was," I confirmed.

"And you and the other PGs were there, right?"

"Right," I replied.

"So, did something happen there, like any verbal or physical fights?"

"Not at all. It was a typical high-school party."

"Yeah, I remember those," she said as she flipped through more of her notes. "Even though you've been with the PGs for only a week, did any of them say anything about someone stalking them?"

"No, not at all. Why would they say that?"

"Well, because they're the PGs. I'm sure they got fans everywhere, but especially at school. Then again, not everyone likes them. I don't wanna include you in any of this since it's only been a week since you've been with them, so this attack on Poppy could've been a stalker of the PGs or a result of someone trying to get revenge on one of them because they feel that they had something to do with Kat's disappearance."

"Yeah, it's possible. But the PGs never mentioned any stalkers."

"Did they mention anything about anyone threatening to hurt them because that person or people feel that they have something to do with Kat's disappearance?"

"No, they didn't," I honestly replied. "All they told me was that they had nothing to do with her disappearance."

"So, did you know of any trouble Poppy personally might be in or has been in?"

"Nothing at all."

"How close are the other PGs to each other?"

"They seem very close since they're always around each other."

"And they will protect each other at all costs, right?"

"That's right."

"They also trust each other, right?"

"That's right," I said again.

"But do you know if that trust could've been violated?"

I shrugged. "I have no idea. I don't think it ever has been."

She kept staring at me. "You may go."

Later on in the evening, I heard my parents talking in their bedroom about what'd happened today and after they had lectured me about it for hours after I'd gotten home from the police station. I stood outside of their door and listened.

"Look, we didn't know all of this was gonna happen in Kitty's first week at her new school. This is crazy," Mom said.

"Well, Gus—Kat's dad—told me that the school revolves around the PGs. They act as if these girls are invincible gifts from God. They get treated better than the athletes there. He said Kat talked all the time about them and how much she wanted to be one of them, now she's missing and there's that infamous picture out there showing her with them and saying that she was last seen with the PGs, even though she wasn't one of them. I just don't know what to think about them having some involvement with her disappearance.

"When I found out that Kitty was hanging with them, I tried to make her think that we were all for it, but now I just don't know how I feel about all of this. Someone hurt Poppy, and I don't know, our baby could be next because of what happened to Kat and someone thinking they had something to do with it, even though Kitty had nothing to do with it since we didn't even live here last year. It doesn't matter. She's hanging with them now so they're all a target. Poppy almost being killed today is proof that not everyone loves them like people claim that they do."

"This is unnerving me, too. I just want our Kitty to be safe, and I just feel that it's just not safe right now for her to continue to go there. Of all schools, it had to be a school like this that worships popular girls but then look what happens to one of them? It's clear that not everyone likes the PGs."

I walked into the room. "Um, I'll be fine at school. I don't think the person who did this to Poppy is gonna come after me."

"How can we be sure of that, Kitty?" Dad asked.

He was right, I couldn't be sure.

"You're right, I'm not. But if me or any of the other PGs stay home then the person responsible for doing this wins, and we don't want that. We want to show this person that we're not scared of them."

But I was scared to death—I couldn't lie to myself—but had no problem lying to my parents which was wrong because they were truly concerned for my safety as they should've been.

CHAPTER 10

"Look, none of us wants be next," Prima said, as we all sat in her bedroom, and her home was so big and beautiful my home could fit right inside of it. "I really believe what'd happened to Poppy happened because people out there are still blaming us for Kat's disappearance, something that we had nothing to do with. But then again, like the detectives who questioned us all said, it could be a stalker who's obsessed with us, but whoever it is, we can't be afraid to go back to school tomorrow."

"But *I am* afraid!" Ariana said. "We don't know who did this to Poppy, that makes it all the more scarier. The cops have no leads on it or anything. Everyone who should've been questioned in this have been questioned either yesterday or today and they've pretty much ruled everyone out."

"Except us," Lauren said with her head down.

We all looked at her.

"What do you mean they haven't ruled us out, Lauren? We should've been the first to be ruled out! Is there something you know that we don't?" Prima asked.

We all kept our eyes glued to Lauren to see what she was going to say.

Lauren sighed. "Prima, you know damn well we haven't been ruled out. People still think we had something to do with Kat's disappearance and it doesn't matter what we say or how many people are supporting us in our efforts to make others believe that we didn't. We all know we had nothing to do with it, but it's clear that from what happened to Poppy that not everyone believes it. I also believe Poppy was attacked probably by one of Kat's friends. It was probably that crazy one, Willa? She's been the most outspoken about us having something to do with Kat's disappearance since she's her best friend."

"I agree," Ursula said.

"Me too," Rika said. "Whether it was someone who thinks we had something to do with Kat's disappearance or a stalker obsessed with us, we're under attack, girls, and we have to face it."

"I'm getting a damn gun," Prima declared.

"Prima!" they all shouted as I shrieked in shock.

"Now I think you're going a little too damn far with that," Olive said.

"You know a better way to protect yourself?" Prima asked Olive.

We all looked at Olive.

"Yes, I do. We have to protect ourselves with knowledge and information. The more we know the better. We can't go around pulling guns and knives out on people if they look like they're about to attack us because if we do then we'll look crazy, and if the teachers or any staff members at school find any kind of weapons on us of any kind then we will be expelled and criminal charges will be brought up on us. We know the school rules so I suggest we follow them for once," Olive said.

"We never really had to follow them before so why start now?" Ursula said.

"Well, we *have* to follow them now," Olive said.

"I think there could be another reason why this happened to Poppy besides Kat or a stalker," Rika said.

"And what is that?" Prima asked.

"Remember how we were harassing those girls who were driving that raggedy car while we were on our way home from that nightclub for teen night?" Rika asked.

"What do you mean harassing *them*? They were harassing *us*—calling us rich bitches just because we were in my mom's Bentley Bentayga. We didn't have to take that shit from them," Prima said.

"We started it, Prima, or at least you did. You yelled down to them, 'Nice car!'" Rika reminded her.

We all looked at Prima. I really wanted to hear more about this since this was before I met them.

"That's because those bitches were talking shit about us at the club the whole night. They knew who we were and they were hating. I'm surprised that piece of junk got them to the club," Prima said.

"But they crashed into a tree on their way back from the club. I feel we caused that to happen to them because the driver couldn't pay attention," Rika said.

"Not our fault," Prima said. "They were seriously hurt but they survived. But that's what they get for talking shit about us."

I couldn't believe Prima was so insensitive about that incident even though I didn't know any of them at the time. And I now had second thoughts about getting into any car and going anywhere with her if she really acted like this.

"Well, I don't think those girls had anything to do with what'd happened to Poppy because they don't go to our school," Ursula said. "This was done by someone or some people who went to our school, and because of where Poppy was found, it was obvious a girl or girls did it, because a guy wouldn't risk going into the girl's bathrooms especially during school hours."

"That's what I think, too," Lauren said.

"Poppy was also known to be a bully to a lot of girls just because she's one of us," Ariana said. "Maybe one of the girls who she bullied got fed up with her and attacked her in the bathroom when no one else was around."

"Sounds possible," Prima said.

The PGs nodded in agreement.

"But the only one who knows who did this to her is Poppy. I can't wait until she's able to tell us," Prima said.

. . .

"This is just too crazy for words, Olive. I can't believe all of this has happened in just the first week that I've been at Sahara Palms and been with you all!" I said, as I talked to her on the phone while I paced back and forth in my room later on after getting home from Prima's house.

"I know this is crazy, Kitty, but it is what it is. I hate for someone like you to come to a new school and have all of this drama happen to you in your first week. You can't even make this up, can you?"

"No, I can't! You know I overheard my parents talking about possibly pulling me out of school because of what happened? But I convinced them that I wanted to stay and that I would continue to go to school. This was an isolated incident—at least I hope it is."

"Yeah, to be very honest, I hope it was, too. I can't shake the fact that Prima is right—we're under attack, and the scary thing is, we don't know who can be attacked in our group next."

"This sounds like a horror movie or something, I can't lie. I think we should always pair up with each other. None of us should be going anywhere alone. I mean, I'm with you all and I have the chance of being attacked by some crazy bitch over who knows what and I haven't done anything to anyone!" I said with clear fear in my voice.

"Calm down, Kitty. I know you're afraid and so am I; so are all of the PGs. We are a target for haters, that's a fact, but I can't say that the PGs didn't put the group in this position."

I found this interesting. "What do you mean?"

"It means that because of our popular status, we've been notorious for being able to get away with stuff most wouldn't be able to get away with. And when they told you about Poppy being a bully, that's just one of the things. I think it was a girl she bullied that beat the shit out of her, and if it was, I'm not saying that it was right, but Poppy should not have been surprised that it happened."

"Yeah, that's true if that's the case. I really can't wait until Poppy tells us who did this to her because I believe she knows."

"Oh, she definitely knows. And she definitely knows if she deserved it or not. Someone wanted to get revenge on Poppy, or maybe wanted to get it on Prima or one of the other PGs and took it out on Poppy because the opportunity was there and the person did it as a message that they were serious about hurting us for who knows what."

"But what is it that you all have done?"

She sighed. "What haven't we done is the question."

"My goodness, Olive. Please tell me. I'm listening."

She sighed once again. "Well, back in September at the beginning of the school year, Prima saw Jaxson flirting with another girl in the class that she was in with him. She walked over to them and started arguing with them and the girl called her a bitch and Prima smacked the shit out of her, I mean she smacked her so hard the girl's face was red for the rest of the day. I was in the class with them, so I witnessed it. The teacher did nothing to her; didn't even report it. I guess some of them really do feel that they don't get paid enough to deal with the shit they have to put up with when it comes to us because teaching is hard enough."

"Wow. And yeah, that's why my parents said they could never be teachers and I said I didn't blame them. I think it's worse for teachers today than it was when they were our age and they said they agree with me."

"My parents also said it's much worse today with what teachers have to put with as well. But everyone heard about what'd happened in class and said that Prima only got away with it because she was a PG. Had it been the other way around then that girl she hit would've been the one who got in trouble for it. She filed something with the school for assault, but no one followed up on it with her, instead, people who worship the PGs harassed her and ran her out of school. She is now enrolled at an online school, I heard."

"Wow," I said as I shook my head. "Prima should've been disciplined for that."

"She should've been. She talks a lot of shit; *a lot* of shit. But that was one of the first times she's actually physically assaulted someone and she didn't get in trouble for it. She told all of us that it was the power of popularity. But to me that was just an abuse of power and that's not how someone should act who had a lot of girls wanting to be her—don't know why. Popularity is not supposed to be about bullying and physically assaulting people and acting all high and mighty and thinking you're invincible to everything that others will get in trouble for, but this is what happens when people put popularity on a pedestal. It's just not right."

"It isn't, Olive. So that's why I'm still so confused as to why Prima let me in the group. I'm none of the things she is. I know she has her good qualities and all of the PGs have them, but the bad ones seem to outweigh the good ones."

"Yeah, unfortunately you're right, Kitty. The PGs have been notorious for their ways, so in knowing this, I'm not surprised at all that this happened to Poppy because she was the second in line to Prima because of the way she acts. Maybe this will wake her up to her ways."

"Well, since I'm still getting to know all of you, have the other PGs done anything that they should've gotten in trouble for?"

"Yes," she replied without hesitation. "Rika is notorious for talking on her phone in class before and after . . . and even sometimes during class. A teacher one day told her to stop talking on her phone because class had started, and she pretended as if she didn't hear him and kept talking. He warned her and she *still* kept talking on it and the teacher was still trying to teach the class despite trying to tell her to stop talking. Rika eventually hung up after she was done talking, but then got out her compact mirror and started refreshing her makeup. The teacher said nothing and continued on with class. If that was anyone else in the class they would've gotten written up for it as well as probably a few days of detention."

"Wow," I said. "I got my phone taken away in the middle of class when I received a text from Zoe. I wasn't actually talking to her during class. There's no way I would get away with that. It's clear that no one cares that I hang around you all. I feel as if I'm treated like everyone else."

"It might feel that way, Kitty, but trust me, you've only been with us for a week, and it's been a hell of a first week, hasn't it?"

"Yeah, it has. I still can't believe it. So, what else are the other PGs notorious for?"

"Well, I can't say much about Lauren because she really hasn't done anything. But I think it's insane that she's still hanging with us when she could form her own group. She seems to be the most decent and nicest one, and I guess in every group you need at least one that is that holds everyone else together."

"Yeah, I could tell that about her. She doesn't seem like the type that thinks she's all that just because she's a PG. I think the other PGs need to learn from her."

"Yeah, they all do," she agreed. "And Ursula, my goodness. Ursula has her moments as well, but she's the type that will go off in a second if someone pisses her off, and she's notorious for throwing shit at people and screaming at them in class. She did that to a guy in her art class who drew a big pair of boobs and said it was the PGs' boobs. He only let his friends see it, but she was behind him and saw it so she started screaming at him and started throwing anything she could find in the class—paint, brushes, pencils, you name it. The class looked like a colorful mess when she was through, and all the teacher told her to do was take her seat and calm down. She should've been sent to the principal's office and got a detention or suspended because that would've happened to anyone else."

"Whoa, that's *crazy*! Ursula is so pretty and sweet with great style. I didn't think she had it in her to act like that!"

"Yeah, looks can definitely be very deceiving. She's done stuff like that before in classes but that was a big, wild mess she made in that class that day. Just don't piss her off."

"I'll keep that in mind!"

We laughed even though it wasn't funny. I didn't see how the PGs could be admired so much if their ways were this bad. It really showed me that being popular had a lot of perks when in these cases it shouldn't, but as long as people treated them like they were "invincible gifts of God" as they said, then their notorious behavior was just gonna go on and on.

But someone tried to put a stop to it, at least to Poppy, but I still felt that what'd happened to her was a message to all of us.

"So, what about Ariana?"

She gasped. "Oh, my God! This one is crazy so I hope you're sitting down for it."

I grabbed my chair and sat down. "I'm sitting now. What happened?"

"Ariana was accused of poisoning an ex-boyfriend of hers that she was with freshman year who broke up with her to be with someone else. It was said that he broke up with her because he said she cared more about being a PG than about their relationship and said that she was not the nice girl she once was in middle school because of it. She didn't deny this, and wanted to make it seem as if she was totally over him—she was far from it.

"Her ex-boyfriend one day got very sick after lunch and was vomiting everywhere, and when they tested him at the hospital, they found traces of poison in his system. It wasn't enough to kill him, but it didn't matter. He suspected it was her and even flat-out accused her, but she denied it all. Principal Harden said that whoever did it was going to be expelled and criminal charges would be filed against them because it happened on school property, but her ex-boyfriend just couldn't prove that she did it even though he was sure she did.

"Later on, she even denied it to us but none of us believed her. She said that if she wanted to try and hurt him or even kill him she would not have poisoned him but would've just shot him instead. To this day, no one has been officially charged with poisoning him, and because of this, he feared for his and his family's safety and left the city. No one knows where they are."

"I think I'm gonna be sick," I said.

And I wasn't kidding. Hearing all of these stories about all of these beautiful girls who befriended me on the first day of school and the way they really were and how much people admired them and all, and they turned out to be nothing but wolves in sheep's clothing, had me scared of them now. I was now afraid to leave the group because of all of the stuff I was finding out through Olive and just hanging with them because I thought they would get suspicious if I did leave, but I definitely didn't wanna end up like Poppy.

I felt that what'd happened to Poppy should've showed the PGs that they were no longer the popular, invincible girls they thought they were, but that remained to be seen.

CHAPTER 11

"My goodness, Olive, the bleachers are packed here, not to mention all of these people standing out in this field. Looks like the whole school showed up for the candlelight vigil for Poppy's recovery," I said.

"Yeah, it does look like it. Remember, Poppy is a PG, so therefore more people are gonna be out here because of it. I kind of wonder if even half of these people would've showed up for an unpopular person," Olive said.

"Yeah, that's a good question, but I think we all know the answer to it," I said.

"Yeah, we do," Olive replied.

It was dusk dark. The light from the candles were now more easily seen, and mine was burning fast. People held white candles and some held green since it was the school's colors. Principal Harden quieted the crowd as Prima got ready to speak.

"Thank you all for showing up here tonight for our friend Poppy Hendrichs. We are all praying for her safe recovery and hope to have her back with us soon because we already miss her not being here. We thank everyone for their support and prayers," Prima said, and then passed the mic to Ursula.

"Like Prima said, thank you all for showing up here tonight. It means a lot to us, Poppy's family, as well as to the school to be showing your support for a Sahara Palm's High School student. Thank you," Ursula said, and passed the mic to Rika.

"Hello, everyone. It means a lot when people show support for a person who loves her school, family and friends. Please continue to keep her in your thoughts and prayers, and we thank you all for coming," Rika said, and then passed the mic to Lauren.

"I know Poppy is gonna see this and it's gonna mean the world to her to have such love and support from her family, friends, and school, as well as the whole community because she loves us all just as much. Keep praying and supporting. Thank you," Lauren said, and then passed the mic to Ariana.

Sounds like they all said the exact same thing, I thought.

"Hi, everyone. I'm glad to see so many people out here when you all could be doing a million other things with your time. This shows how important you feel that this moment is, and we feel it with you. So thank you all for coming out to support Poppy and keep those thoughts and prayers up," Ariana said, and passed the mic to Olive.

Olive stared out into the crowd. "Wow. I've never seen a vigil like this. Like Lauren said, when Poppy sees this, it's gonna mean the world to her, and I know this is gonna give her all of the strength and confidence in the world to get back to where she knows she's loved. Thank you all for showing all of your love and support for our friend," she said, and passed the mic *to me!*

Oh, no!

I didn't know I would have to speak!

I stood frozen with fear as the microphone felt like a twenty-pound weight in my hand. To make matters worse, my candle was almost burned to the bottom and I felt my left hand getting hotter than it already was. I looked at my parents who were standing in the front row. They nodded back at me and smiled, and that was their way of saying that it was going to be okay.

Just what the hell was *I* supposed to say?

"Uh, hi, everyone. I'm Kitty Laine. I'm new here at Sahara Palms."

Everyone stared back at me like they wanted to say that they knew

I was and to just say what I'd planned to say. But this wasn't planned. I didn't know Poppy long enough to say anything about her, but when I thought back to what each PG said, they didn't say anything about her personally either. They kept it short and basic and to the point, and I felt that was what they wanted me to do.

"Um, I've only been here for a week and on my first day here, the PGs befriended me. I'm so glad they did. I see just how much love and respect people really have for a student here, and we should show that kind of love and respect to all students here and to all people in general. I didn't wanna even fathom the thought of losing such a great person so fast, and now I don't have to because she will be back with all of us all thanks to the power of support and prayers. Thank you all."

Everyone finally clapped as I quickly passed the mic back to Principal Harden. My parents smiled at me and gave me the thumbs up. I smiled back in relief.

I opened up the door to my car and was about to get in.

"I wish this many people would've showed up at Kat's vigil."

I turned around.

It was Zoe!

She was wearing a black baseball cap and glasses, as well as dark clothes. I didn't even recognize her at first.

"Zoe, hi. I didn't see you out there."

"I was there. I just stood back from everyone else. I didn't want too many people to know I was here. I actually walked here since I don't live too far away. Can I have a ride home so we can talk?"

I looked around to see if the PGs were anywhere in sight. They weren't. "Sure, get in."

"Were you serious when you said that you were glad that the PGs befriended you on your first day?"

I felt awkward saying it now, especially since I didn't know she was at the vigil. "I felt uncomfortable saying it, I'll admit that. Please don't tell anyone."

"I'm not," she promised. "It's just that I know they did something to Kat and we talked about it, so I was kinda shocked that you said that."

"I was honestly blindsided by having to speak. I didn't think they were gonna pass the mic to me because like I said, I've only been at the school for a week so I couldn't say anything about Poppy personally, so I kept it short, sweet, and to the point like all of them did."

"Yeah, I kind of figured that. I knew by the way you stood up there with the mic in your hand that you were shocked that they were making you speak. You should've told the crowd not to forget about Kat."

"I didn't wanna cause any trouble."

"I know, Kitty, I was only kidding." She sighed. "Kat's vigil wasn't nearly as big. We had it in the park in our community and everyone was invited. There were probably less than a hundred people that showed up, and as you saw, it's a pretty big park so it could've held a lot more than that. And no, the PGs did not show up. Not even one of them. People just don't care about people who aren't popular it seems."

"Now don't say that, Zoe. If people didn't care about Kat then the posters and flyers all around school wouldn't be there. People do care."

"Not as much as they should. I know this shouldn't be a competition, but they said Poppy is gonna make it. I don't even know if Kat is still alive. I can't help but to think that it was someone who cared about Kat that hurt Poppy. I'm not saying it was right if they did."

"Um, don't tell anyone this, but the PGs were saying that it could've been Kat's friend Willa who hurt Poppy."

She grinned. "Willa may be crazy at times, but I don't think she's that crazy where she would do something like that. She can't stand the PGs, but said she wouldn't risk going to jail over hurting one of them. And she was questioned in Poppy's incident, all of Kat's friends were. Someone obviously wanted to hurt Poppy bad or maybe just one of the PGs and she just happened to be in the wrong place at the wrong time. If this didn't have anything to do with Kat's disappearance then it could've been a million other reasons. Not everyone likes them, in fact, I think more people hate them than like them."

"It's looking that way to me too. I'm just scared, Zoe, I really am. I don't wanna have to be looking over my shoulder constantly at school when I hear someone walking up behind me and thinking they're gonna attack me. That's no way to live. Never in a million years did I think my first week at Sahara Palms was gonna be like this."

"No one could've predicted this, Kitty. You walked in on some fucked-up shit, that's for real. And now you're with a notorious group of girls who act as if they're freakin' angels but they're anything but that. It's just unbelievable to me how a group of chicks can become so popular and worldly famous for doing absolutely nothing but being rich, pretty, and having great style. They're the true definition of wolves in sheep's clothing."

I pulled up in her driveway. I looked up at the window that had pretty lavender lights shining through it. "Your room has pretty lights."

"That's Kat's room," she informed me.

"Oh, I'm so sorry," I replied as I lowered my head in shame.

She smiled. "It's okay, Kitty. At night, we keep her lights on in her room. Her room is in the exact condition that it's in since she's been missing." She opened the door. "Will you let me know if the PGs talk again about her? I know they all have Poppy on their mind so I don't expect them to talk about her at all right now, but if they do, let me know, okay?"

"Okay."

"Thanks for the ride home."

"You're welcome."

I watched her as she walked up to her house and walked inside.

Minutes later as I drove down the road, someone came up fast behind me. They flashed their high-beam lights more than once, signaling for me to pull over. It was dark so I didn't recognize the car. I figured it was someone who knew me, so I pulled over with extreme caution. I made sure both of my doors were locked and fumbled through my purse to look for my can of pepper spray.

Tap, tap, tap.

I looked up and it was Olive! I breathed a sigh of relief and rolled down my window. "Olive. You scared me. I didn't recognize your car since your lights were so bright."

"Sorry I scared you, Kitty. What were you doing at Kat's house?"

I tried not to show any shock. *What were you doing following me?* I thought. "I was giving Zoe a ride home. No one knew it, but she was at the vigil."

"She was? Wow, I didn't see her," Olive said. "Well, if you wanna come back to my house so we can talk about this more then you can. My parents aren't home."

"Are any of the other PGs gonna be there?"

"No, they're not. They said they just wanted to go home after the vigil and chill. It's been a long day."

"It has. But I'll see you at your house."

CHAPTER 12

"Wow, fresh popcorn is the best! Your popcorn machine is so cool," I said, as we sat in the family room of her house eating popcorn, candy, and drinking soda.

"I can only eat like this on the weekends," she said, and then downed a handful of popcorn. "Oh, and I'm sorry I passed the mic to you earlier. I know I freaked you out when I did that."

I laughed. "You did but it's okay. It would not have been right if all of the PGs spoke and I didn't. I just didn't know if I should've said something about Poppy because I'm still getting to know her like the way I'm getting to know all of you, but now I'm glad I did speak."

"We're glad you did, too," she said with a smile. "And actually, none of us had that planned. Prima just passed the mic to Ursula and she passed it to Rika and on it went until it reached you. I think everyone wanted to hear from us so it was actually good that Prima did that."

Not for me it wasn't, I thought. "Yeah, it was."

"Oh, I keep forgetting to ask you since this has been a hellish week and especially for you. It's obvious that you never heard of a blog called The Popular Girls, huh?"

"No, I haven't. I assume that this blog is talking about you all?"

"And you now as well."

"What?!"

"Calm down, Kitty. They haven't said anything bad about you, it's just that now since Prima let you into the group you're gonna be talked about. It's inevitable. People have done videos about us and everything, but this blog is still one of the most popular blogs in the world. We have no idea who's writing it about us because they're obviously remaining anonymous. It could be one person, could be several and we're thinking that it is because they say 'we' and 'us' a lot; they could go to our school or not, we really don't know. They've been writing about us since freshman year and always refer to us as PG and then our name, which you know PG stands for Popular Girl, so you'll always see your name as PG Kitty on it when they speak about you or any of us. Prima loves it because it's brought even more attention to the group, and the others love it as well, but not when they say bad stuff about us because they've done that, too."

"Can I see it?"

"Let's go to my room and look at my computer so you can see it better."

She pulled it up on her computer. "Here it is. And I see they already have something written about Poppy's vigil tonight."

I stared at the picture that they had of the PGs on their front page, and I was included in this picture. It was one taken at Brennen's party that he took of all of us. I actually liked the picture and felt like I was officially a part of the group. I read what they said:

THE POPULAR GIRLS
UNDER ATTACK
THOUSANDS TURN OUT FOR GET-WELL VIGIL FOR
PG POPPY

How many girls in this world would have thousands of people
pack the high-school stands and football field for a girl who's
only known for being popular? Popularity definitely has its
perks! We were the first to report on the beating of PG Poppy,
and still no one knows who did it.

The pictures were gruesome, so we could imagine how she looked in person to the girls who saw her. We don't wanna seem like a gossip blog but that is what we are, and all of us here are wondering what led to Poppy getting beaten within an inch of her life. She's very lucky she survived and we're all thankful for that because we're not the type that believes someone should get beaten like that, but there are a lot of unanswered questions as to why what went down did.

The PGs each spoke to the crowd, but we had to laugh when Olive passed the mic to new PG Kitty because she looked like a deer caught in the headlights of an 18-wheeler semi-truck! But we could understand because she didn't know much about Poppy since she's only been with the PGs for a week, and we know it's been a hell of a first week for her.

But how much do the other PGs know about Poppy is the question?

Poppy was hurt this bad for a reason, and we're trying to find out everything we can about why she was and who did it. Some say it has a direct connection to Kat Black's disappearance, but we don't wanna say anything unless that's confirmed. Some say she's notorious for being a bully, and that's been confirmed. But it could be a million reasons since she is a PG, so we hope that the other PGs stay safe because we don't want our next story to be about another one of them being attacked because all of them have notorious ways!

I instantly became obsessed with this blog. This was one of the most popular blogs in the world and I could see that with them having over a million views and thousands of comments, and I was not going to read though them all—but I was curious about some of them. I was now a part of this blog and it was inevitable that I was going to be talked about a lot on here. I didn't know if I could handle all of this already, but I had no choice but to do the best I could.

"I don't have any notorious ways," I said.

"Neither do I or Lauren," Olive said. "But see what I mean when it's one or a few then it's all of us."

"Yeah, I see that. But that's not right because I feel that we're our own person, we just have different personalities, but it seems to work out since we're all friends in the same group. I guess you all were looking for someone very different so I was chosen, huh?"

"Well, Kitty, Prima and the rest of them had been talking for a while about adding someone to the group whose name didn't have to spell out popular and I think they preferred someone new. And it was perfect that you're new to the school."

"I guess I had great timing, huh?"

"You absolutely did!"

We laughed.

"Yeah, that's funny that they said that I looked like a deer caught in headlights because I do. It even looks funnier when I see myself in these pictures."

"There's video of it as well," Olive said with a grin.

"Do I wanna see it?" I laughed.

"Only if you want to!" she replied with a laugh.

"Yeah, why not? I've never seen anyone get me on video that I didn't know. I've only been on family videos."

She turned it on and I burst into laughter at myself because I looked like what everyone said I looked like—a deer caught in the headlights of a semi-truck!

"Okay, I got my laugh for the day!"

"Glad to hear it," she said with a smile.

And it was good to laugh, but underneath the laugh was fear and a lot of it. I just felt that I couldn't relax until we found out who did this to Poppy.

CHAPTER 13

"What do you mean we're not on the approved list to see her? We're her friends! What the hell?" Prima said while talking on her phone outside in the school parking lot after school. "Yeah, whatever." She hung up.

"Why won't they let us see her?" Ursula asked.

"They wouldn't tell me," Prima replied.

"This sucks. I mean, her parents need to do something about this. Look how many people showed up at the vigil and we, the ones who are the closest to her, can't see her?" Ariana said.

"Is she in any condition to be seen yet? It hasn't been that long since this happened, so her parents probably don't want anyone to see how she looks," Lauren said.

"I have no idea, but we all saw her lying there in that bathroom. That was the worst condition she was in at that point. She can't be in any worse condition than that," Prima said.

We all nodded in agreement.

But I was wondering why we couldn't see her because I really wanted to because I knew she knew who did this to her.

"Well, we have no choice but to wait," Olive said.

"Yeah, but for how long? We shouldn't have to wait as long as the others," Rika said.

"I know we shouldn't," Prima said as she shook her head as her phone hung by her side. She looked at her phone. "Fuck off!" she said, and pounded her finger down on her phone.

"Who was that?" Ursula asked.

"I have no idea. Probably some stalker who got a hold of my number. Have any of you been getting any texts from people you don't know?"

"Yeah, I've been getting some," Rika said.

"I seem to always get them. I just delete them and block them," Ursula said.

"Same here," Lauren said.

"Yeah, I admit that I have as well. I try not to let them get to me," Olive said.

"Me too," Ariana said.

Prima looked at me. "Kitty?"

"Not yet," I replied.

"Well, don't hold your breath because they're probably coming just so you know," Prima warned me.

"I'll let you know if they do," I said.

At home, I couldn't do my homework. My obsession with the PG blog was in full effect:

THE POPULAR GIRLS
UNDER ATTACK
THE PGs ARE DENIED HOSPITAL VISIT TO SEE PG
POPPY—NO REASON GIVEN

Well, this is quite interesting! We found out today that Poppy's beloved PGs were blocked from being able to see her and was not given an explanation of why. Prima was told that she, nor any of the other PGs, were on the approved list for visitors.

Prima tried to keep her cool and all, but let it all out when she told the PGs about it.

What the hell is going on here?

Why wouldn't they be allowed to see her yet?

When we asked the hospital about this, they said they didn't have any comment only except to say that Poppy is in fact allowed visitors, but her friends were not allowed? What kind of sense does that make?

It's clear that there is a reason why they weren't allowed to see her, and we will soon find out!

I had to admit I was wondering that as well. I had to agree with this blog because it didn't make any sense that we hadn't been able to see her yet. Maybe Lauren was right, maybe her parents wanted us to see her when her condition was better, but she absolutely could not have been any worse than what she was when we first saw her . . . or maybe there was another reason.

CHAPTER 14

"This is boring," I said, and closed my American Government book. I was over Darius' house studying with him since this was one of his favorite subjects.

He laughed. "It's okay, Kitty. Not everyone feels the way I feel about it. We can take a break and just talk."

"Yeah, let's do that," I wholeheartedly agreed.

He laughed again. "So, what do you wanna talk about?"

I shook my head. "There is so much to talk about, but I just don't know if I should be talking about it."

"Well, whatever you wanna talk about I won't tell anyone about. I know you're with the notorious PGs, so any secrets you tell me are safe with me."

I looked at him. "Do you really think they're that bad?"

"Actually, I don't. I know they're not angels, and you know how I feel about Lauren, but it doesn't seem like she acts like the others."

"No, she actually doesn't so you picked the right one to have a crush on."

He laughed once more. "That's great to hear."

I sighed as I stared down at my closed book.

"Kitty?"

I looked at him.

"I'm listening."

I sighed again. "Everything is still bothering me. I didn't expect any of this at all being at the school for only a few weeks now. This is just crazy. But it feels like I've been there for a few years. Everything just seems like it happened so fast and it seems like the PGs have a connection to every damn thing that goes on. Now one of us is hurt and they say she should be able to go home in another few weeks, but it's like her parents won't let us see her."

"Yeah, I heard about that. Have you found out why?"

"No, we haven't. That's the thing. There was the huge vigil for her and we all spoke at it and then we find out just a few days later that we're not on the list to see her? And she does have it where people can visit her."

"Yeah, that doesn't sound right. I'll see what I can find out at the hospital, one of my aunts is a nurse there."

"Oh, wow, that's perfect, Darius! I was hoping someone had some kind of connection to the hospital where she's at. If you find out anything, can I tell the PGs?"

"I don't see why not."

"Um, just between us, who do you think could've done this to Poppy?"

He grinned as he sat back in his seat. "I honestly don't know, Kitty. She was notorious for being a bully, so maybe a girl that she bullied finally got revenge on her. I don't like to speculate that much about it since the only one I've ever talked to this much about the PGs is you, but that's really all I can think of."

"You don't think her attack had something to do with Kat's disappearance?"

He shrugged. "I don't know. But it's possible."

I sighed. "Yeah, it's possible. I just feel like we're all going in circles with this. Nothing seems to be enough to break any of these cases wide open. It's just that now I'm all wrapped up in it and I feel that I can't move forward until we know who's responsible for both things."

"It could be several people, or it could be the same person for both. You just don't know and none of us will know until we find out the truth."

"And I hope we're not waiting forever for the truth."

CHAPTER 15

"This is bullshit. It's been another week and they're *still* not letting us see her? All they tell us is that her condition is improving each day. Has Darius been able to tell you why we can't see her yet, Kitty?" Prima asked me as we walked to our cars after school.

"No, not yet. He—"

Prima and the rest of the PGs screamed to the top of their lungs!

And I could see why.

All of their cars had their windows broken and their tires slashed!

And on both sides of all of their luxury white cars had the words "Killer" and "Liar" put on them in black spray paint.

I ran over to check my car . . . and it was perfectly fine.

"WHO THE FUCK DID THIS TO OUR CARS?!" Prima yelled to the top of her lungs. All she got back in response was shocked stares, glares, and complete silence. "SOMEBODY KNOWS SOME-THING! TELL ME!"

Silence.

The rest of the PGs looked at their cars in disgust as they got on their phones to call someone, and I was assuming their parents or the car dealership, or even the cops. I was amazed that no one did anything to my car, and I felt that the only reason they hadn't was because they either didn't know which one it was or that they knew I didn't have anything to do with what was going on with the PGs.

The PGs were definitely under attack, and even though no one did anything to my car, I was right in the middle of it.

"Wow, Kitty. Someone or some people really hate your new friends," Dad said, as he cut his steak. "I'm just glad they didn't do anything to your car because that was some extensive damage those vandals did."

"And I'm glad they didn't, either. This was done to them by someone who thinks they had something to do with Kat's disappearance. I can't think of any other reason," I said, and then ate some more of my corn.

"This is just crazy," Mom said. "How the hell was someone able to get away with vandalizing *six cars* in broad daylight? Where was the security?"

"There isn't anyone who patrols the student parking lot from what I know. I guess they think the school is in a safe neighborhood and aren't gonna waste money on hiring anyone to do it. I honestly think it was someone who went to our school, then again, the PGs are worldly known so it could've been anyone, and with all six of their cars being vandalized, it definitely had to have been more than one person. I just don't think one person could've did all of that alone. But this is crazy, Mom, like I've been saying since I've been there. Now I'm gonna have to hear it for I don't know how long about this and who they think did it."

"Looks like you need to find a new group of friends already," Dad said.

"It's not the PGs, Dad, it's the people who are hating on them that are doing this. They are under attack because of Kat's disappearance and I believe Poppy was the start to it. They all even agreed that what happened to their cars was nothing compared to what happened to Poppy, but it's still all bad and it just needs to stop. I haven't had anything done to me but I feel like I have and it might be all a matter of time before I do."

"That's why I don't want you hanging around them anymore. They seem to have more of a bad rep than a good one," Dad said.

Mom looked at me.

"It's all of the haters that are making their rep bad now. I really don't think they've done anything that bad to have these bad things happen to them. No, they're not perfect angels but no one is. I just want to find out who was involved in Kat's disappearance and who tried to kill Poppy because I believe now that someone did try to kill her."

"I've been saying that all along," Dad said.

"Aaron!"

"Sorry, Carol, it's what I believe. I just didn't wanna have you upset, Kitty."

"I am upset, Dad. I'm upset about all of this. This is supposed to be a fun time for me since I'm at a new school and a junior, but all it's been is drama after drama."

"Do you wanna go to an online school?" Mom asked.

Dad looked at me to see what I would say.

"No way, it's not for me. I was given a chance that no other girl would've gotten on her first day at a new school, and that was to hang with the popular girls. I really need to stick it out with them because I consider them my friends. I just hate everything that's going on right now with them. I honestly don't think they deserve any of this, especially Lauren and Olive."

"No one deserves to have what Poppy had done to her as well," Mom said.

"Yeah, you're right, Mom. And I just don't know if any one of us are next. I can't help but to think that my car was not vandalized because the person or people didn't know which one it was."

"And thank God they didn't," Dad said.

"I said the same thing," Mom said.

"So did I," I said.

And I meant it. I felt so bad for the PGs, and I was determined as much as they were to find out who did this.

THE POPULAR GIRLS

UNDER ATTACK
PGs' LUXURY CARS VANDALIZED IN STUDENT
PARKING LOT
"KILLER" and "LIAR" SPRAY PAINTED ON DOORS

Okay, someone or some people are definitely out to get the
PGs, and it's getting even uglier now that someone or some
people are sending a strong message to them that they're not
invincible to bad things happening to them just because of their
popular status. We think that the person or people who are
doing this to them definitely have some kind of score they
wanna settle with them, and that they're winning by a landslide.

The PGs have also said that a lot of them are receiving threatening text messages from unknown people as well, and this has
been happening since Kat's disappearance but is really
happening a lot more than it was before. Also, with Poppy
being attacked, no one really knows what is going on here and if
the physical attack on her is tied to Kat's disappearance or
something else.

Or are all of these attacks on the PGs tied to something we all
don't know about?

"Killer"

"Liar"

Interesting choice of words that were put on all of their cars.

This person or people obviously knows something that the rest
of us don't know, or are they full of it?

Kitty's car was the only one not vandalized, and we believe it's
because she's new and has nothing to do with the notorious
ways of the PGs . . . yet.

Well, we think we'll find out soon because we all hate to say it and think it, but we don't see any of this ending anytime soon.

"Yeah, neither do I. I feel that if it's really gonna get worse, I might have to reconsider my mom's suggestion about me going to an online school because I'm trying to stay strong, but if I start getting attacked over stuff I had nothing to do with then I'm outta there."

CHAPTER 16

"YOU ALL LOOK FABULOUS. I WISH I CAN SHOP THE WAY ALL OF YOU do," I said to the PGs as we all walked toward the exit doors of the mall. I had only one bag from Forever 21, but the PGs had all kinds of luxury bags from Neiman Marcus, Saks Fifth Avenue, Louis Vuitton, Chanel, as well as a lot of others—at least three to four different bags in each hand—and I saw just how depressing it actually was to shop with a bunch of girls who never had to shop on a budget.

"Thanks, Kitty. Maybe one day you will. That's why you're hanging with us so you can see how it is to be able to shop like a pro and for the best stuff. You see how all of us are wearing something new. We always make that a shopping tradition to walk out of at least one store wearing or carrying something we just bought," Prima said.

"All of your new outfits and bags and shoes are stunning," I replied.

They all gave me their many thanks.

"Yeah, it's nothing like a fabulous shopping trip to lift our spirits!" Ursula said.

All of the PGs nodded in agreement.

We left out the doors when we were suddenly stopped by four people wearing black ski masks and dark clothes!

"THE BLOOD OF KAT BLACK IS ON ALL OF YOU!" they yelled.

They threw red paint on all of us and ran off!

We all screamed in horror as we stood in shock at what'd just happened to us. I felt like I was in a nightmare and I knew that the PGs felt the nightmare continued for them as well.

Now this was personal. These people physically attacked *me*. Now I really felt that I was a part of the PGs.

The PGs stood screaming and crying in the police station as the front desk officers tried to calm them down. I just wanted to go home and take a shower. Luckily, unlike the PGs, I was wearing something I'd had for years, and luckily it wasn't a favorite tee or jeans or sneakers. But the PGs all had on brand-new, very expensive outfits and some were even carrying new bags and wearing new shoes, and now all of those pretty things were completely ruined by a bunch of red paint by people who had no proof that they had anything to do with Kat's disappearance and didn't know whether or not she was still alive.

"Okay, girls, *please* calm down, okay? Someone will be with all of you to take a report of your incident," one of the officers told us. But I could tell that it took everything out of him not to laugh at us covered in red paint, but it actually wasn't funny at all.

Minutes later, I sat in a room and in walked the same cop who interviewed me about Poppy, Detective Jennifer Markson.

"Kitty Laine. Wow, you and your friends are going through a pretty bad time right now, huh?"

"Yeah, we are. But I don't know why I was targeted in this latest incident because I had nothing to do with Kat's disappearance. The PGs told me they had nothing to do with it and I believe them."

"Well, it's clear that four people think the PGs had everything to do with it."

"But *I* didn't! I wasn't even there at the time this happened. I didn't even know who the PGs were around this time last year."

"I know, Kitty. It's unfortunate that you end up at a school with some of the most popular girls in the world and because of their notorious ways, you end up having stuff done to you as well. It's not fair at all, but it's a true meaning of guilt by association."

"Yeah, I should be the poster girl now for that. I just didn't think nothing else would happen because I'd been a week or two since their cars were vandalized. Now I really don't think any of this is gonna stop until they find the real people responsible for Kat's disappearance, and who the hell knows when that will be."

"Yeah, we don't know, Kitty. We just don't have any leads on it. So, you can't describe the four people who did this?"

"No, I really can't. It sounded like two boys and two girls. They were of all heights and some were skinny and some were slightly over-weight. It's clear that they're pro-Kat, as Prima and the rest of the PGs say. They were completely covered. I think they probably go to our school but then again Kat's case made international news because of the PGs alleged involvement so it could be anyone."

"Yeah, you're right, it's hard to tell."

"But like I said to the PGs, now I have to take this as personal as they're taking it because this was a direct attack on me as well. It's not like they told me to get out of the way so they could just throw it on all of the other PGs and not on me. They know I'm new to the school and the PGs befriended me. I mean, what the hell was I supposed to do? Say I didn't wanna be friends with them? That would've been crazy because I didn't have one friend going into the school that day. Some-times I do have to wonder how all of this would be had I never went to the bathroom that morning and didn't crash into Prima in there because the floor was slippery."

She grinned. "Well, there's nothing you can do about it now except maybe find new friends. None of this is your fault, Kitty, and I would hate to see you have to put up with all of this when if there is anyone who can walk away from it all, it's you."

I stared at her when she said this. She was right. I was the only one who could really walk away from all of this because I had no involve-ment in any of it, but for some reason, I just didn't think I could get myself to do it.

. . .

Hours later, I stared at myself in the bathroom mirror after taking a shower. I unwrapped my towel from my head and checked to see if I'd gotten all of the red paint out of my hair. It looked like I did. I had to give the clothes that I wore at the mall to the cops so they could do what they did about having them tested and everything, but I felt that the only way those four were gonna be found was if somebody snitched on them because people definitely knew who all four them were.

I sat down at my desk to look at the PG blog, and sure enough, they had their story about it:

<u>THE POPULAR GIRLS</u>
UNDER ATTACK
RED ALERT!
PGs GET "BLOOD" THROWN ON THEM AS THEY
LEFT THE MALL!
"THE BLOOD OF KAT BLACK IS ON ALL OF YOU!"

Okay, we shouldn't be laughing about this, but the pictures looked funny of the PGs standing outside of the mall looking shocked as they should've after four obviously pro-Kat supporters splashed them all with red paint, ruining their brand-new outfits that they just bought that day. Unfortunately, Kitty didn't escape this latest incident unscathed because she, too, was splashed with the red paint even though she didn't even know the PGs when Kat disappeared last year.

But how do they know or anyone know that Kat's no longer alive?

Throwing "blood" on someone is saying that the person is dead, at least that's what we think and we're sure that's what everyone else thinks, too.

The PGs did file a report with the police and are now safely at their homes, our sources told us. Poor Kitty. She had nothing to do with this and now she's all up in it as well. If we were her, we would find some new friends! But nothing beats being with the PGs no matter how tough times get and they're pretty tough right now! We still believe it's how Kat got in trouble because she tried her hardest to be one and they never accepted her.

We contacted Zoe, Kat's sister, about this latest incident, and she told us that the only person she felt sorry for is Kitty since she had nothing to do with anything. We have to agree with her on that. If you're reading this, Kitty, we would love to hear from you so you can contact us if you wish to do so about how you feel about being caught up in all of this mess when you're still considered new to the school and to the PGs. What a hell of a time you're having!

"Hell is not even the word to describe this. I don't even know what to call it," I said in response to this latest post.

My phone rang. I looked at it and saw that it was Olive.

"Hey, Olive. How are you?"

"I'm hanging in there, Kitty. I had a hard time trying to get that red paint out of my hair, and a new Alice + Olivia outfit of mine is ruined because of the paint, but other than that I'm fine."

"I'm so sorry that this happened."

"I'm sorrier for you since you had absolutely nothing to do with this."

I thought what she said was interesting and I really didn't think she realized what she'd said. "Well, I had nothing to do with it just like you didn't because you weren't with them last year, either."

"Yeah, I know, but it's clear that I'm still a target and unfortunately you are as well. It's because we're a part of the group."

"I wish people would just leave us alone."

"Yeah, me, too. But it's clear that it's easier said than done. I wish I would've known the four who did that shit because I have to agree with Prima, I don't know if I would be able to hold my composure."

"Yeah, you're not the only one. Now I'm taking it personal because they messed with me. I'm seeing firsthand now what you all are really going through."

"Yeah, you are. But they had no right to do that to you. I'll always stand by that."

I smiled. "Thanks, Olive. So, did anyone know if Poppy knows what happened today?"

"I'm not sure. I think her parents are keeping a lot from her because she doesn't wanna upset her."

"Oh, okay. That's understandable. She's been through enough."

"She sure has."

"Oh, did you see what those bloggers wrote about us?"

"Of course. We all admit that we're obsessed with looking at it because all they do is talk about us. I honestly don't see the fascination, but it is what it is. We just got lucky to get this popular. It was nothing that we did to be this way."

"That was something I did wanna know."

"It was just our social media presence and all, but most of all, it was luck. I don't think we would be this popular had it not been for social media."

"Yeah, a lot of people wouldn't be. But as people see, it's not all what it's cracked up to be."

"Absolutely not. Sometimes, Kitty, I just feel like walking away from it all. Don't tell anyone I told you that."

"Oh, don't worry, Olive, I won't. So just the PG status makes you stay, I assume? Even though they're known for being notorious?"

She sighed. "Yeah, it is. I admit that we have brought stuff on to ourselves, but it's never been this bad where someone went missing, we're accused of it, and people are trying to hurt us because they think we had some involvement in it. We already lost one PG, and now Poppy is in the hospital because someone attacked her and we still don't know who did it. I just can't fathom losing anyone else."

"I can't either. That's why we all need to stick together and continue to be strong for Poppy and for ourselves. I believe all of this will be over once the people who are truly responsible for both incidents are caught and I believe all of these people who have been committing these personal attacks on us will stop as well."

"I really hope so, Kitty."

I looked at my text messages on my computer and a text popped up from Zoe. "Olive, I have to go. Talk to you later."

"Okay, Kitty."

I texted Zoe back and told her to call me.

"Hey, Zoe. I'm glad you called me because I really need to talk to you."

"Yeah, I know, Kitty, and I need to talk to you as well. I just want you to know that I was not one of the four people who did that to all of you today, that's why I wanted to make that really clear with that blog that it was not me, and I meant that when I said that the only person I feel bad for is you because you're the only innocent one in all of this."

"Thank you, Zoe. I was hoping that at least someone would see it that way, but the cop that I'd talk to today was the same one I first talked to about Poppy's case. She said it was guilt by association, and I can't help to think that she's right."

"Yeah, unfortunately, she is. And even though I didn't do it, I didn't put those four up to doing it, either. I feel that even though I know the PGs have something to do with Kat's disappearance, I just feel that doing stuff like that is unnecessary and it just creates more problems."

"Yeah, it does, and just to warn you, the PGs vow to get revenge on whoever did it. They were all wearing new outfits and some of them even had new bags and shoes. It almost seemed as if they cared more about their stuff getting messed up than what was done to them. I'm scared, Zoe, I'm not gonna lie. I don't want any more shit to happen—excuse my language."

She chuckled. "It's okay, Kitty. I swear a lot more than anyone thinks I do. It's just that it's almost been a year since Kat disappeared and her case hasn't gotten anywhere. I feel the PGs have everything to do with it, so I don't see how they can walk around at school and everywhere else as if they have no idea what happened."

"Maybe they really don't know what happened, Zoe. Have you ever thought about that? There's no proof that they did anything, even though that picture of them with Kat suggests otherwise to many people. I think people are only accusing them because of their popular status and notorious ways as everyone says. They may have done a lot of things, but maybe this isn't one of them."

She sighed. "I try so hard to get myself to believe that, Kitty, but I just can't. Kat wanted to be one of them so bad, and I feel that she was just not gonna leave them alone until they let her in their precious, prestigious little group, and you know I'm being as sarcastic as I can be when I use the words precious and prestigious."

"Yeah, I know you are."

"I just feel like they snapped on her or something. I honestly don't think the PGs are ever gonna tell the real story and I feel they have already gotten away with this. They have too much popularity and that equals power, so I know people are just not gonna waste their time always questioning them about it."

"Well, are there other suspects to consider?"

"Like who?"

"Like any boys like Brennen since he was Kat's boyfriend?"

She sighed once again. "Brennen was definitely questioned, but I honestly don't believe he had anything to do with her disappearance. He got into a lot of fights with Kat about her obsession about wanting to be with the PGs, but I don't think it was enough to make him do something horrible to her."

"I hope not. Well, did she have any other guys she was seeing behind Brennen's back?"

"Not that I know of. If she did then she never told me. There might be another suspect out there if that's the case and if it is then it's like we'll be starting all over with the investigation."

"I really feel so bad for you, Zoe, and your family for having to go through this. I know a lot of families go through this that have missing kids, it's just not fair."

"It's not, Kitty, but it happens and unfortunately we're one of the many families that this has happened to. It sucks. It sucks bad. And it's unfortunate that the suspects happen to be the most popular girls not just at Sahara Palms, but the most popular in the world. They have more support out there than we would ever have. They have power and status. They have mind control over others. It's like they can say anything they want about anything and people will believe what they say because they're the PGs. Most girls in this world would kill to be like them. And I honestly think Kat was almost to that point."

"Oh, goodness, I really hope not. I will always say that no one, and I mean no one, should wanna be in someone's group that bad that they will do something so awful to be in it. It's like people in gangs killing innocent people just to get in them. It's just awful, just awful."

"Yeah, you're right, Kitty, it is. But remember what I said about the mind control. I believe the PGs have that over so many people. It's like people are under their spell or something. If they say they didn't do something then they didn't do it and people should just automatically believe them, and a lot do. Some people just have that, and the PGs are one of them."

"Yeah, that's really unfortunate."

"But fortunately, I have someone like you who is on the inside with them, and I still trust you that you will tell me if they ever talk about what happened to Kat, right?"

"Exactly right, Zoe."

"And no one knows that we're talking, right?"

"Right," I lied, since only Olive knew, and I wasn't so sure if she'd told any of the other PGs.

"I can honestly say that I think those four people who splashed you all with red paint this afternoon only did it for attention. They could be pro-Kat, but then again maybe not. You know people will do anything for attention even though they didn't show any of their faces. It's just something about it."

"Yeah, but they did it at my expense when I didn't even do anything."

"I'm sorry again, Kitty. I can't say it enough."

"I know you are, thanks."

I always felt good talking to Zoe, and felt so bad that I had nothing to tell her in regards to the PGs mentioning anything about Kat when I'd talked to her like this. I just hoped the next time someone thought about doing something to the PGs because they believed they had everything to do with Kat's disappearance that they would leave me out of it.

CHAPTER 17

 her dad, Nate,
said.

"About what?" she asked, as she was about to go downstairs.

"Just come to our bedroom," he said.

Prima walked into the suite area of her parents' master bedroom.
"Look, I really don't wanna talk about this."

"Too bad because we're gonna talk about it," he informed her.

"We just don't want this stuff to keep happening to you and the
other PGs," her mom, Priscilla, said.

"Well, we all know why it keeps happening because people are out
there still talking about us being the ones that had something to do
with that girl being missing," Prima said.

"Look, dear, we know you all had nothing to do with that, but this
is really unnerving your dad and I because it looks as if these attacks
on you all are starting to happen every other week. You already lost a
PG to suicide and another one is in the hospital still from being badly
beaten. Then, you all had your cars vandalized, and now red paint
thrown over you all. We just wanna know if there is something you're
not telling us," Priscilla said.

Nate looked at Prima to see what she was going to say.

"There's nothing to tell about anything because we didn't do anything," Prima said. "I'm not lying to you both. People only think we had something to do with it because of that stupid picture. That picture means nothing because we definitely weren't the last ones seen with that girl like everyone thinks we were."

"Why are you degrading her by calling her 'that girl,' Prima? You know what her name is. Would you like it if people referred to you like that if you were missing and still haven't been found in almost a year?" he asked.

"No, I wouldn't, but no one would refer to me like that anyway or any of the other PGs. We're loved by almost everyone, and yeah, I know the reality is that not everyone loves us that's why I say almost. The motherfuckers who did that shit to us today obviously are some our biggest haters."

"Watch your mouth, young lady!" Nate said with anger. "You know we didn't raise you to have a potty mouth, even though your mom has one."

"Look who's talking?!" Priscilla said with anger.

"All right stop! I'm already mad enough and I'm sorry about swearing, Dad, but they ruined my brand-new outfit, bag, and shoes. That stuff was expensive!" Prima whined.

"Yeah, it may have been, but I could think of a lot of worse things those four could've done to all of you instead of just ruining your clothes and accessories, so consider yourselves lucky," Nate said.

"Yeah, we are," Prima conceded.

"And how is Kitty doing in all of this? I know the poor girl is the most innocent because you all didn't know her when that girl went missing last year," Priscilla said.

"She's doing as fine as she can do. She's still upset about it like the rest of us. We all had a FaceTime conference about it almost an hour ago. I honestly didn't think all of this would happen to us when I chose her to be a part of our group on the first day of school. I wanted someone like her to have the All-American high school experience since she was new to the school, and there was no better girls that she could hang around than us."

"You're right about that, darling," Priscilla said.

"Oh, please," Nate said as he rolled his eyes. "I'm sure Kitty is having a lot of second thoughts now since all of this crap has been going on with you all, huh?"

"Actually, I asked her that and she said she still wants to hang around us because we befriended her when no one else would. She knows she can't get any better than us."

"Don't flatter yourselves," he said.

"It's not flattery, Dad, it's the truth. Every girl wants to be us so I'm just stating facts."

"I'm sure not anymore since all of this crap is going on with you all. You all have been accused of doing some pretty notorious things, but never did I think my own daughter would be accused of another girl's disappearance," he said.

"We had nothing to do with it and I will always stand by that and the rest of the PGs will as well," Prima said. "Whoever is doing all of these bad things to us just wants to see us miserable because they're not us, but we're very strong young women and we will continue to get through this."

"And that's what I love to hear," Priscilla said with a smile.

"And I hope you all stay strong because I don't see an end to any of this anytime soon," Nate said.

"You both can count on it," Prima said.

Ariana sat on her bed as her older sister, Adriana, talked to her about what'd happened to her today. She was home visiting her family for two weeks.

"Ari," Adriana said, since this was what she called Ariana for short. "Mom and Dad wanted me to talk to you now since they're still out tonight with friends. I'm glad I'm at home for two weeks so I can talk to you in person and not through texts or social media because this just needs to be discussed in person."

Ariana looked at her. "What needs to be discussed in person, sis?"

"What happened to you and the PGs today," Adriana replied, as she gave her a very serious look. "And let me not forget Kitty. I'm sure she was very traumatized, huh? Considering the fact that a lot of people are blaming you all for Kat's disappearance, the attackers should not have targeted her."

Ariana shrugged. "Well, she's the one who agreed to hang with us so she should've known that all of the stuff that we're involved in will unfortunately involve her, too. Look, I do feel bad for Kitty because she didn't know what she was gonna be getting herself into with having to deal with all of us. There's always drama with us because everyone either wants to be like us or hates us, and Kitty is right in the middle of it. I know that what's been going on in these past few weeks with us has been stressing her out as much as it's been stressing me and all of the other PGs out, and I can't blame her. Like Prima said, we wanted her to have the All-American high school experience, and it just doesn't get any better than that than hanging with us."

"Well, don't blame yourself or the PGs for all of this, Ari. I know that you couldn't predict all of this shit that's been going on with you all and I know that Kitty couldn't predict none of it. But if it keeps up, what are you gonna do?"

Ariana gave her a confused look. "What do you mean what am I gonna do?"

Adriana sighed. "Look, Ari. You have to really think about what happened to you all today, okay? You were all very lucky that you survived it. What those four could've done to all of you could've been much worse. People are crazy out here. They think they're some vigilantes of some sort—I don't know. I know there's no proof that you all have anything to do with Kat's disappearance, but that's not how people see it. They always want to be all up in other people's business and all when it doesn't concern them, and with all of this social media and the connection people feel like they have to everything, it's just that some take shit too far when they should just stay out of it. I think that's the case with those four as well as whoever had something to do with beating up Poppy. I think they tried to seriously kill her, Ari, and that scares me."

"It scares me, too. I even told the PGs that. I'm scared to go anywhere now, especially to school. I'm scared to be anywhere by myself. I just don't know when any one of us could be next, but look what happened? We were all attacked at the same time today. I just don't see this getting any better for us."

"I don't think so either, Ari." She let out a deep sigh. "I just think that maybe you should think about removing yourself from all of this crap because if you don't think it can get any worse than this, well, it could and it more than likely will."

Ariana looked at her like she just couldn't believe what her sister was saying. "Are you telling me that I should think about *leaving* the PGs? Are you serious?"

Adriana continued to stare at her. "You know what you need to do."

"NO! No way! Are you *crazy*?! The PGs is who I am! I wouldn't be anything without them! Prima changed my life that one day when she let me into the group! Why would I all of the sudden leave her and the rest of them because of all of this shit that's been going on? We survived what happened to us today, okay? And we survived everything that has led up to it and we will survive everything else that comes after it! We're stronger together and that's how we're gonna stay! If we start to break apart then we're fucked, sis! We're fucked! That's *not* gonna happen to us! It's just not!" she cried, as tears flowed down her eyes.

Adriana reached over to Ariana's nightstand and gave her a box of tissues. "I didn't mean to upset you, Ari, you know that. I know how much the PGs mean to you. I saw how you seemed to have changed overnight not just physically, but emotionally and mentally as well. Since I'm two years older than you, I saw how fast the PGs were emerging to be one of the most popular groups in the school, and now not only are you all are, you're the most popular high-school girls in the world. It definitely means something, Ari, but it doesn't mean that your life should be constantly put in jeopardy because of it."

"I agree with you, sis. I just wish that all of this shit would stop, too. I'm gonna tell you something, though, that I haven't told the PGs or Kitty. Since what's been going on has, I've been constantly thinking back about my pre-PG life, you know? Sometimes, I hate to say it, but I miss that pre-PG life. I just miss the fact that I was unknown because when I was, I was able to blend into the crowd and be a naturally private person. But all of that changed when Prima asked me the question that all of the girls wanted her to ask them—would I be interested in being a part of their group. No girl alive would've turned it down, I don't care what a lot of them would say."

Adriana nodded. "Yeah, you're right, they wouldn't!" she laughed. "I have to say that you all are much, much more popular than my group of high-school friends at the time, in fact, you all almost outdid us!"

"And, sis, that's another reason why I wanted to be a PG—to impress you since you were a part of the most popular group at our school at the time. I had the rare chance to be a part of the popular group in my grade so I took that chance and I haven't regretted it since, but now given what'd happened to us today and it could get worse, I just don't know what to think anymore."

Rika sat at the kitchen table with her mom as she whined to her about how her new outfit and shoes were permanently ruined from the attackers throwing paint all over them.

"Rika, *enough* about that damn outfit and shoes, okay? They're just material things," Rika's mom, Rumi, said. "Your dad was worried sick about what'd happened to you and was ready to fly all the way back here from South Africa tonight to be here for you until you told him directly that you were fine. You being a PG is the reason why you're in this mess right now."

Rika sighed. "We are going through hell right now, Mom, okay? But all of the PGs admitted that these are the times that we really need to stick together. Our sanity is definitely being tested, and we all definitely could've lost it today. When a group of people run up to you with masks and dark clothes on, it's not because they wanna shake your hand."

"Yeah, you're right about that," Rumi said, as she shook her head.

"But I'm still here. All of the PGs are here and so is Kitty."

"Poor Kitty," Rumi said. "She's such a nice girl. The time when you two were here studying for your class, she was just so polite—like she didn't want to do anything wrong."

Rika smiled. "She is a nice girl, Mom. It's too bad that she's been caught up in all of this crap with us. But we all think it's gonna come to an end really soon especially when they find out who's really behind Kat's disappearance and who beat up Poppy."

"And that can't be soon enough," Rumi said.

Ursula came out of her bathroom with her bathrobe on and hair wrapped up in a towel after getting out of the shower to her parents waiting for her in her bedroom. "What?"

"You know *what*, Ursula," her mom, Lana, said.

Ursula sighed. "What do you both want me to say about it?"

"Say that it's clear that what's going on with the PGs is obviously getting out of control," her dad, Rodney, said.

Ursula shook her head and sat on her bed. "Well, we can't help it that people wanna hurt us over something they can't prove. This is how people are, Mom and Dad. They're obviously pro-Kat and think we're getting away with something that we're not. Look what happened to Poppy? Those four probably had something to do with it. We're looking at things very closely now because if we overlook one incident then we can start overlooking others and so on and so on and this crap that's going on with us will never stop. Just like how all of these people out here think we're suspects in Kat's disappearance, we think they all had something to do with sending us threatening texts, vandalizing our cars, and now throwing red paint on us like it was blood. I even think they hurt Poppy. No one is not a suspect to us."

"Do you two ever think about what you started here?" Rodney asked, referring to the other person being Prima.

Lana looked at her. She then looked away since she always encouraged Ursula and Prima to start the PGs.

"Dad, there's nothing wrong with what we started. It's not a hate group or anything like that and everyone knows that. We couldn't predict how popular we've gotten—it even went beyond our wildest dreams. But people hate on us and that's a fact, and now they're just being more active about showing it, all thanks to social media. Yeah, we've been pretty wild in our ways, but we've never hurt anyone, so I don't know why the hell all of these people out here are trying to hurt us and has hurt one of us," Ursula said.

Rodney shook his head. "Ursula. I sure as hell hope you or the other PGs are not going around making threats to people on social media because you all *think* that they're the ones who are doing all of these things to you all."

"We haven't made any threats to anyone, Dad," Ursula let him know. "It's just that this needs to stop because it's not cool at all. Whosever doing this to us is just jealous of us and thinks we got away with something that they think we're guilty of when we're not. We didn't think that anyone would go this far in wanting to hurt us, but now we know that they don't want to hurt us, they want us dead. Look what happened to Poppy? Any one of us could be next!"

"I think that all of this has gone way too far," Rodney said. "I'm gonna have to talk to the cops about this."

"Well, I hope you do because we all want this to stop, but they keep saying they have no leads on anything. I care about the PGs, not about anyone or anything else," Ursula cried.

"Well, you should care about the girl who's missing, Ursula," Rodney said.

"Yeah, I do hope she's found, but I'm tired of all of us getting blamed for why she's missing and look at all of this crap that has happened to us because they think we're responsible for her missing? I'm tired of it. I'm tired of all of it. I don't think her or her family would care about me or any of the other PGs if one of us were missing."

"Well, if she's found alive then you can ask her that," Rodney said.

"No thanks," Ursula replied.

Lana and Rodney looked at each other and then looked at her.

Lauren sat in her dad's office in front of his desk as her mom sat in a chair next to her.

"I don't have to tell you how lucky all of you got today," her dad, Tyler, said.

"No, Dad, you don't. I think it goes without saying," Lauren said, as she sat with her head lowered.

"I just don't understand all of this, Lauren," her mom, Marla, said. "You told us at first that you all were safe, despite all of the previous stuff that's happened to you all and especially after what happened to Poppy."

"Mom, I hate to say it, but we're not safe, none of us are. People are really upset about what's been happening to us, but no one's doing anything to help us stop what's going on because I have to be honest, I think this thing is bigger than we have to admit that it is."

Her parents gave her a look of interest.

"Can you elaborate?" Tyler asked.

"That's just it, Dad, I really can't. Something just seems strange about all of this. I do believe that it's some pro-Kat people doing this, but I think some people are putting people up to doing all of this, or maybe these are different people acting on their own," Lauren replied.

"Well, I want all of this foolery to stop," Marla said.

"I agree," Tyler said.

"Well, that's just it, Mom and Dad. Once people have their minds made up about someone or some people being suspects in a disappearance, it's very hard to change it. We're seriously minding our own business because we have no reason to mess with anyone. We stick together no matter what and this is the time when it's really tested. We all could've been killed today instead of having fake blood thrown on us because when they approached us looking the way they did I thought they were gonna shoot us. But you see how we're all still here because we were meant to all still be here and be together. We have to be here not because of us being PGs, but because we have a hell of a lot to look forward to, and you know I'm not saying that no one else doesn't."

Her parents smiled at her.

"And we hope you all find out who's doing this to you all and I just hope that it stops because I don't want you to end up like Poppy," Tyler said.

"Oh, we're gonna find out, Dad, we will!" Lauren pledged. But deep down inside, she wasn't so sure if they ever would, and she'd never told the PGs or Kitty about her uncertainties.

Olive's entire family stood right in front of her as she sat alone on a couch in the family room. She sighed. "I feel like I'm going through an interrogation."

Her family continued to stare down at her.

"Olive, *you know* I was against you being with those girls from the start, and that's because I know what the PGs are really about," Olive's mom, Jolie, said.

Olive sighed. "I know that, Mom. Look, I love being a PG, okay? Yes, they're known for their notorious ways, but it's not like it's all been bad being with them."

"They're accused of Kat's disappearance, Olive, and you decided that you *still* wanted to be a part of their group and especially after Olivia committed suicide?" Odessa, Olive's sister, asked.

"If I thought they had anything to do with Kat's disappearance then I would've never joined their group. I was not there that night so I don't know anything. And I don't know why Olivia committed suicide, okay? But the PGs told me that she had a lot of problems and was mentally unstable at times. But despite all of this, being a PG is the best thing that's ever happened to me. No, it wasn't right for me to leave my old friends to be with them, but my old friends weren't the best of friends, either. I always felt like I was the odd girl out when I was with them, but with the PGs, I feel like I really belong with them."

Odessa shook her head. "Well, if they felt like you belonged with them then why didn't they pick you to be with them from the start? You were a replacement, Olive, all because of Olivia's suicide."

"I cringe when I think about that," Olive's dad, Percy, said.

"Me too," Jolie replied.

Olive shook her head. "That had nothing to do with me. I've never asked them why they picked Olivia over me, okay? And I'm not gonna ask them. I'm with them now and I'm staying with them. Like I said, for once in my life I feel like my life means something by being with a group of girls that people love and respect, and yeah, I do know that we're not loved and respected by everyone out there—and what's been going on with us proves that—but the majority rules. As you all know since you all follow me on social media that I'm never rude or disrespectful to anyone, and that's how you all raised me to be. Just because I'm a PG doesn't mean that I've really changed."

"Well, the other PGs need to change because there's a reason why all of this shit keeps happening to you all and you know what they say," Percy said.

Olive looked up at him. "What, Dad?"

"That bad things always happen to the nicest ones," Percy replied, as he gave her a serious look.

"Dad!" Olive cried. "Why are you trying to scare me? As if what happened today didn't scare me enough?! These bad things are happening to *all of us,* including Kitty. It's really messed up right now, but like how we all said when we all talked earlier through FaceTime, things will get better and that these are the times when we really have to stick together."

"Well, I just think you should give more thought to who these PGs really are, Olive, and what you've gotten yourself into by being with them. People just don't do things to people unless it's warranted, and we've seen the nasty stuff you all have done and said to people, so what's been going on with you all should not be a surprise," Jolie said.

Olive sighed. "Mom, *please.* I know that the PGs are not the nicest group of girls, and my niceness never gets a chance to show through all of the meanness that the PGs permeate, but they're not mean all the time. I don't like it and tell Kitty that all of the time. I'm actually known for being way too nice to be a PG, and so is Lauren, and now Kitty is as well. But I told Kitty that the group needs some niceness so that's one of the reasons why we're in it.

"The PGs love being mean because they know they can, and it's like the people who like us love it—don't know why, but they do. The group definitely needs an attitude makeover, that's for sure, and I think that started by them letting Kitty be in the group since she was new and had no friends, but I don't run things so I really can't say much."

"Well, you better speak up about how they need to change their ways before it's too late," Percy said.

Jolie and Odessa nodded in agreement.

Olive sighed once again as she looked at her family; they stared back at her with very serious looks on their faces. They meant every word, and she knew it.

CHAPTER 18

"Today marks the one-year anniversary of Kat's disappearance. As of today, we still have no reputable leads and have no signs of her anywhere. We can't even say where she was last at or who she was last seen with, and we all know that there have been speculations in terms of what I'd just mentioned, but I don't wanna get into that tonight. Tonight is Kat's night, that's why I'm standing with you all today and seeing firsthand that everyone out here and everywhere else still has not forgotten about her. My family and I thank you all for being here tonight. Hopefully, another year won't go by and we're still not any closer to knowing her whereabouts. Keep up the hope and keep up the prayers for her safe return. Thank you," Zoe said, as she stood with her family and Kat's friends by her side along with about a hundred others. Each person held a pretty lavender-colored candle—Kat's favorite color—in her honor.

I stayed in the back away from everyone. I wore a baseball cap and a different pair of glasses that were my backup pair just in case I lost or misplaced the pair I wore every day. I smiled as people stood around and talked while holding on to their candles, and it was great to see that even though it'd been one year since Kat's disappearance, people still cared and wanted her home.

"Hey."

I turned around and looked right into Zoe's eyes. "Hi, Zoe. I hope you don't mind me being here, because, you know."

She smiled. "Yeah, I know. I almost didn't recognize you. Do they know you're here?"

"Not at all. And I would appreciate it if you don't tell them."

"You know I don't talk to them so you don't have to worry about that."

I breathed a sigh of relief. "Thank you."

"Wow, I can't believe it's been a whole year since she's been gone. It just seems like a year went by so fast, then again it seemed like the slowest time. I mean, me having to pass her room every day and thinking that she's in there, or thinking that each time the phone rang or one of the doors opened to our house or I heard a car coming up the driveway, I thought it was her. I even thought each call or text I got on my phone was her, but it wasn't. I even found myself throughout this past year calling and texting her and never getting a response. Is that crazy for me to do?"

"Not at all, Zoe. I expect for loved ones to do that. I don't have any siblings, so I honestly don't know how you feel."

She nodded. "I didn't think you did. My parents told me they do the same thing as well. I think it's just us not giving up hope that she will answer our calls or texts someday."

"And that's the positivity any family needs is to never give up hope. I think no news is good news."

"That's what we're all saying as well. I just wish someone had more information about all of this, but the right information. I'm sorry that I hinted to your group as being the ones that people are speculating about being suspects. I didn't know you were out here until just a few minutes ago when I got a better look at you."

I looked around. "Do you think anyone else out here recognizes me? I just didn't wanna be noticed since I do hang with the PGs."

She looked around as well. "No, I actually don't think anyone knows it's you, Kitty. Sure, everyone knows who you are because you hang with the PGs, but I don't think anyone recognizes you here."

<u>THE POPULAR GIRLS</u>
FAMILY MEMBERS OF KAT BLACK HOLD ONE-YEAR
ANNIVERSARY VIGIL FOR THE STILL-MISSING
SAHARA PALMS HIGH SCHOOL STUDENT
SISTER ZOE SPEAKS AT VIGIL
UNEXPECTED PERSON SHOWS UP AT VIGIL SEEN
TALKING TO ZOE

Okay, everyone. We were all over the Kat Black one-year
anniversary vigil that was held in the family's gated community
park where they live. And we knew Zoe was not going to be
short of words there, but stopped short of directly accusing the
PGs of having something to do with her sister's disappearance.

It's hard to believe that it's been a full year since Kat's been
missing, and since there has not been any confirmation of her
no longer being alive then we can all assume that she very well
could be, and that's what we're all hoping for.

But one of us got an interesting picture of Zoe talking to a girl
who looked a lot like PG Kitty, but we can't confirm whether or
not it was her because she had her hair covered in a baseball cap
and had different glasses on—but it sure did look like her to us.

If it was her, it's clear that she has a serious interest in this case,
and if she did show up with all of the pro-Kat supporters
around, that was very brave of her to do considering the attack
on her and the other PGs when they left the mall not too
long ago.

But, Kitty, if that was you, we'd love to hear from you to
confirm it because we got a lot of questions to ask you, so give
us a call or text or send an email. We'll be waiting to hear
from you!

"Shit!" I said. "And I thought I covered myself good. Now I'm gonna have to come clean to the PGs about this and why I was there. I can't believe I'm all caught up in all of this and I had nothing to do with any of it."

My phone rang.

It was Prima.

CHAPTER 19

really you in this picture talking to Zoe at Kat's vigil tonight?" Prima
asked me, as she shoved her phone in my face.

I wanted to run out of my own bedroom. And here I was, supposed
to be safe in my own house and especially in my own bedroom, sitting
in a chair at my desk as the PGs stood over me and stared me down,
waiting for my answer.

"Well?" Prima asked.

"Yes," I squeaked out with my head lowered.

The PGs shook their heads in disappointment.

"Why, Kitty? What the hell were you doing there?" Prima asked.

"I just wanted to see what they would say," I honestly replied.

"Why do you care what they say?" Ursula asked.

"Yeah, why do you care, Kitty? You weren't even here when this
happened," Ariana said.

I sighed. "I'm sorry, PGs, but I do care. I have to care. Look what's
been done to all of you as well as to me now because of it? I just
needed to see if anything would be said at it that hasn't been said."

"Was there anything said about us?" Olive asked.

The PGs continued to stare at me.

"Not that I know of," I replied.

"What? Kitty, that's not an answer. You were there, weren't you?" Prima asked.

"Yeah, I was, but I might have missed something so I'm not sure," I replied.

"I think someone has it on video," Lauren said, as she checked her phone. "Yeah, someone does. In fact, there are a few videos of it already." She put her phone up as all of the PGs gathered around to look at it. I stayed put. She turned her phone off when the video was done.

"Well, it's clear that Zoe was saying it without saying it that we've been suspects from day one. That chick better stop talking about us like this and I mean it or she's gonna regret it," Prima said.

"Kitty, is Zoe making you spy on us or something?" Rika asked.

"That's what I wanna know," Prima asked as she stared down at me.

"Yeah, we all wanna know, Kitty, so tell us," Ursula said.

I looked at each one of them as it was clear that they really wanted to know as if their lives, as well as mine, depended on it. "No," I finally said. "And I'm not lying to you all. I'm not spying on you. I went there on my own will. I didn't have anything to do tonight and just wanted to hear what was gonna be said there like how I said before. Zoe is not having me spy on all of you. What's going on with you all is going on with me as well, and I wasn't even here when all of this shit happened."

"Well, I'm sorry that you're going through all of this with us, Kitty, but we're all friends, remember? So we all have to stick together like what friends do when it comes to this, and the last thing we need is to have any of us turning on each other. Now is especially not the time," Prima said.

"I still don't trust Zoe," Ariana said. "I still think she's wants to be close to you, Kitty, just to get you to tell her what we all say about Kat. As you know, all we have told you is the truth, we had nothing to do with it."

"That's right," the PGs said.

"And I have to believe that as well because she feels that she can get through to you, Kitty, rather than someone like me because you're new. Remember, I wasn't with the PGs either a year ago so she could be trying to talk to me about it but she hasn't even tried," Olive said.

"That little chick will do anything to try and get us in trouble over this. I know she sent her little 'Kat Kult'—as we call them—to come after us. I know they're all responsible for all of the shit that's been happening to us, and like how we can't prove who's responsible for all of these attacks on us, she can't prove we're responsible for Kat's disappearance," Prima said.

"That's right," the PGs said once again.

Prima paced in my room. "Kitty, I really didn't wanna have to do this, but I think I'm gonna have to."

I stared at her. "What is it, Prima?"

Then, a horrible thought hit me. Something that I wasn't expecting but then again it would've woken me up to the reality of really being with the PGs.

I was about to be kicked out of the group.

"I hate to be a bully about this because Poppy is the real bully in this group, but I'm gonna have to say this," she said. She stopped in front of me and looked me dead in the eyes, and something about it sent chills all through me. It even looked demonic. "I'm gonna have to tell you to stop talking to Zoe and that starts right now, so you need to erase her contact info from your phone and block her from contacting you."

I kept staring at her in disbelief. She was serious, they were serious. Yeah, she was being a damn bully, and now I was really seeing how they actually acted. I was warned about how they were, but now it was personal. "Okay." I got my phone off of my desk and deleted Zoe's information . . . but I didn't block her.

"Good girl," Prima said. "Your allegiance is to us and no one else. Remember who befriended you on your first day at your new school and first-period classes hadn't even started. When we say we didn't have anything to do with something we didn't have anything to do with it. We just don't want any outsiders trying to poison your mind with their lies because no one knows what happened to Kat except for Kat."

And the last person or people with her, I thought. But I didn't wanna say anything now. I felt degraded and embarrassed that Prima forced me to do this like I was the bad person for just wanting to pay my respects to a girl who we all didn't know whether or not we would ever see again.

But I had to admit I was glad I wasn't kicked out of the group because I honestly didn't know what I would've done if I was. There were a lot of things going on and it was getting scary, but I vowed to find out . . . everything.

"Kitty, I'm so sorry Prima made you do that in front of everyone. That was so wrong and embarrassing," Olive said, as we talked on the phone later that night.

"It was, but I really didn't think it was wrong for me to attend Kat's vigil. I just wanted to pay my respects. It's not like I'm friends with Zoe. She has every right to be the way she is, and I wasn't lying about the fact that she's not making me spy on you all."

"I believe you, Kitty. I can't believe it's been a year already. But there's some info I found out about the case before you even got to our school that I haven't told anyone about."

I sat straight up on my bed. "For real, Olive? What is it? And how come you haven't told anyone?"

"Because I'm not sure if it's credible, Kitty. Just remember when this happened I wasn't with the PGs either, so I can't confirm anything."

"You haven't said *anything* to the PGs about it?"

"Hell naw, I haven't. I don't wanna upset them because you see how fast they can get upset and you don't wanna get them too upset because you don't know what could happen."

"Yeah, that's what I'm afraid of. So, what is this info that you found out?"

She took a deep breath. "This has to stay between us, okay?"

"You got it, Olive."

She took another deep breath. "I was told that there was a fight between one of the PGs and Kat—a physical one. I don't know where this happened at, but it didn't happen at school because the whole school would've known about it and there would be videos of it everywhere."

I shrieked! "What? Oh, my God, Olive! Do you know what the fight was about?"

"I have no idea, Kitty. That's really all I know. I'm not sure if this is credible or not, it's just something that someone told me. I'm not sure when this happened, but I'm assuming it happened the day she disappeared or the day before she disappeared—not sure. Like I said, don't say anything. This is one of the reasons why I don't think the PGs are being a hundred percent truthful about having absolutely nothing to do with her disappearance."

"This is getting even more scarier than it already is, Olive."

"I know it is, Kitty, and you have every right to feel this way. Like I said, this information seems credible because of Kat wanting to be a PG so bad and they just got tired of her. But this fight supposedly happened with *one* PG, not with all of them."

"I think it was with Poppy," I said.

"It's possible, but why do you say her?"

"Because she's in the hospital. Maybe someone obviously wanted to finish what they started for Kat. I know it sounds crazy, but it could be true."

"It's very possible, Kitty, but then again the person who originally said this could be full of shit, and I have no idea in the world who originally said this, of course, because the person told me about it said they saw it on social media, and you know how fast shit gets around on there. We'll just have to see. As you see, the PGs aren't talking, and it's interesting how Prima will put a gag order on you not to talk to Zoe anymore about it. Why would she do that if they didn't know something about the case? This is rubbing me the wrong way as well."

"Well, Olive, since it seems like you're the only PG that I can really talk to and trust, this has *always* rubbed me the wrong way."

"As it should."

"And now since you told me what you'd told me, I didn't wanna say this, but there was a girl in the bathroom on that very first day at school that told me not to have lunch with you all. She was actually in the stall when I was talking to you all. All she told me was not to have lunch with you all but didn't tell me why. She just abruptly left before I could ask her any questions."

"Have you seen her since?"

"No, I haven't. It's clear that I didn't listen to her because I had lunch with you all and now I'm still hanging with you all despite everything that has happened since I've been here."

"Yeah, I think it was someone who was trying to scare you into not talking to us because of Kat's disappearance. If you see her again, point her out to me."

"I will."

CHAPTER 20

It was Principal Harden. And if he was interrupting classes with an announcement then it was pretty serious, I even knew that at my other school. And a principal interrupting the middle of classes with an announcement was in most cases was not good.

Lauren and I looked at each other as we sat in Business Writing and braced ourselves for what this announcement was gonna be about. I looked around the rest of the room and the tension was very thick. A lot had been going on, and it was clear that there might've been some news about it that we were not gonna be prepared to hear no matter how much we thought we were.

"I want all of the students and staff here to know that Poppy Hendrichs, a junior, has been released from the hospital this morning and is back home with her family," Harden informed us.

"YES!" Lauren yelled out loud in class.

Everyone nodded in agreement with her.

"We're going to see her today, Kitty!" Lauren informed me.

"Can't wait," I replied with a big smile.

. . .

"What the hell do you mean we're not allowed to see her?" Prima asked, as we all sat in one of her mom's SUVs, the one that was big enough to hold about ten people in it.

"I'm just saying what I was told," the security guard informed us. And he looked like a no-nonsense type of man; I thought Prima was crazy for trying to argue with him. "You're not on the list of approved visitors. The Hendrichs family gave us a strict list of people who were allowed in here and I don't see your or any of your friends' names on the list. Sorry, you'll have to leave. You're holding up the line."

Prima screeched off as I held on tight to the door handle. I was scared to be in the car with her now. "Girls, I don't know what is up with this shit about how her family wouldn't let us see her at the hospital and now that she's at home? This is really making me mad!" she said, and turned a corner at a fast speed without even slowing down to stop.

"Prima, there's obviously a reason and we will find out, okay? But could you please slow down? You shouldn't drive when you're mad," Lauren said.

"I agree," Olive said.

"Me too," Ariana said.

"I don't care!" Prima barked at them.

"You're too upset to drive, Prima. We're all upset, but let one of us drive, okay?" Rika suggested.

"NO!" Prima yelled and turned another corner very sharply, almost sending the SUV on only two wheels.

"STOP IT!" Olive yelled. "You're not gonna kill me or any of the rest of us because you're pissed off, Prima! Slow the fuck down!"

"Shove it!" Prima said, and ran through a red light!

We all screamed!

I felt like I was in a nightmare. Us not being able to see Poppy had her very upset, but I didn't want my life put in jeopardy because she was so mad about it. I didn't deserve this and neither did any of the rest of us.

Sirens suddenly went off!

The cops!

"Shit!" Ursula said, who was sitting up front with Prima as she looked back in the back window of the SUV like the rest of us. "You better pull over, Prima, he obviously saw you run that red light!"

Prima amazingly pulled over and screeched to a stop, which jerked us all forward. Luckily, all of us were wearing our seat belts. "Shit! I can't find my damn license and registration—oh, here it is," she said as she pulled out both things. She glared at the cop as he came up to the window.

"Good afternoon, I'm Officer Vince Baldwin. Can I see your license and registration?"

Prima sighed as she handed it to him. "Why was I pulled over?"

Is she serious? I thought.

Olive and I, as well as the rest of the PGs, all looked at each other.

"You ran a red light," he informed her. "And you were far enough back to make a safe stop. Are you in a rush to get somewhere?"

"No," Prima replied.

"So why did you run it?"

"I'm just mad right now, okay? All of us are," Prima replied with an irritating tone in her voice.

"Well, you shouldn't drive when you're mad. Should've just pulled to the side and calmed down. Or let one of your friends in here drive if any or all of them have a license. They don't seem upset to me," he said, as he looked in at all of us; we all smiled at him in return.

"They are," Prima informed him.

Don't speak for us, I thought, and knew the other PGs were thinking the same thing.

"I'll be right back," he informed her, and walked away and back to his car.

"I should drive off," Prima said.

"Are you freakin' crazy, Prima? Don't even say stuff like that!" Lauren said.

"Not with me in the car you're not!" Ariana said.

"Me too," Olive said.

"Me as well," Rika said.

"She was just kidding, girls. Right, Prima?" Ursula said.

Prima stared ahead and didn't say a word, and this sent chills through me. I wanted to get out of here and call one of my parents to come pick me up or have the cop take me home.

The officer came back up to Prima's window with all of her information and a ticket. "Slow down and don't run anymore red lights. You could've seriously hurt yourself, your friends, or someone else. Have a nice day, ladies."

Prima slowly pulled off and threw the ticket in the glove compartment. "I'm not even looking at that shit."

I didn't even wanna imagine how much that ticket was.

"I don't want you in a car with that girl anymore if she's driving, Kitty. She could've hurt or even killed one of you, some of you, or all of you doing what she did this afternoon," Dad said, as we sat at dinner.

"I was scared, Dad, I admit that. I didn't know she was gonna be that upset about not being able to see Poppy. It seems like it's been so long since we've seen her. I was even thinking we were gonna be able to see her today since she's now at home, so I think anyone could understand why we were upset that we were denied entry to the community that she lives in. I'm just not understanding this."

"Neither am I," Mom said, and ate some of her rice. "What is really going on in your group, Kitty? Because this does seem strange that one of the girls gets hurt and her family has completely cut you all off from seeing her."

"Mom, if I knew then I would tell you. That's why Prima was so upset."

"Yeah, and her little butt shouldn't have been driving if she was that upset," Dad said. "You know we taught you that and driving school taught you that."

"Dad, I know. Even the other PGs were telling her that she should not have been driving when she was mad, and Rika even suggested that one of us drive, but Prima wouldn't let us and I could understand that because the car didn't belong to any of us. But I was scared, I'm not gonna lie. Prima just seemed to turn demonic after she was told we couldn't see Poppy. I wanted to jump out of the car and just call one of you to come get me."

"Yeah, you should've," Dad said.

"Well, if it would've gotten worse then yes," Mom said. "Sounds like the cop saved y'all from something bad happening if Prima would've kept that up."

"I think he did. I didn't think she was even gonna pull over at first, but when she did, I felt relieved. She was even talking crazy about how she was gonna drive off while we were sitting there waiting for the cop to come to her window."

"Now she would've been a fool to do that, and if she did, I would've made sure you never spoke to her again," Dad said.

"I was hoping that she wouldn't, and I'm glad she didn't. I knew how mad she was but was hoping she wouldn't do anything that crazy, but it sure felt like she was going to!"

Dad and Mom grinned as they still ate.

I was glad to be telling them this, but this had me scared of Prima because I'd seen firsthand how she acted when she was mad about something, and she didn't wanna listen to any of her friends for her own good. But what had me wondering most of all was why we still weren't allowed to see Poppy now that she was at home. It was clear that she was well enough to go home, but she wasn't well enough for us to see her yet? None of this made any sense, but I was determined to find out what was really going on.

After I was done with my homework—and I was willing to do it to get my mind off of Prima's crazy driving earlier—I checked out the PG site:

<u>THE POPULAR GIRLS</u>
ROAD RUNNERS!
PRIMA BLOWS THROUGH RED LIGHT IN BIG, BUSY
INTERSECTION THIS AFTERNOON AND GETS
PULLED OVER BY THE COPS!
WHAT WAS THE CAUSE BEHIND HER MADNESS?!

Okay, everyone. We admit to being obsessed with the PGs, and we have people everywhere so we don't miss out on the latest happenings with the most popular high-school girls in this world. And well, it was clear that Prima and the PGs went to pay PG Poppy a visit at her home in an exclusive guard-gated community, but was turned away. We still don't know what was said because the security guard did not wanna provide us with any details, but we learned later on it was because they were flat-out denied entry in there to see her. Since the guards can only let approved visitors in there, it was rumored that none of the PGs were on the list to see Poppy.

None of them.

What is going on?

And this is obviously the reason why Prima was so mad and it explained her reckless driving which led her to blow through a completely red light in a huge, busy intersection and get pulled over by a cop and rightfully so. She did end up with a ticket, so it was clear her popular status couldn't get her out of it and it should not have. It was also said that she didn't put up a fight with the cop and didn't go on a "Do you know who I am?" rant like what was probably expected of her. She was obviously very mad!

But seriously, her madness could've hurt her and the other PGs as well as other innocent people, but if this is true about the PGs being turned away from seeing Poppy when she's at home safe and sound, the million-dollar question is why?

"Yeah, that's what I would like to know, it's what all of us would like to know."

My phone rang; it was Olive.

"Hey, I know what you wanna talk about," I said.

She laughed. "Yeah, you do! Sorry if I'm always bothering you, but believe it or not, Poppy was the one I was the closest to before this happened to her. I just looked at the PG site."

"So did I."

"And yeah, I really wanna know why we're not able to see her. She's who she is because of the PGs. Her family are being jerks about this. I just don't think this is fair. I know they wanna keep her safe, but we're not the enemies."

"I know we're not, Olive. This is making no sense to me. It's clear that Prima is really upset about this and I can't blame her. First the hospital, and now this. But she didn't have to put her life and our lives in jeopardy with her reckless driving because of it."

"I one hundred percent agree with you, Kitty. My parents were really mad about it when I told them. They even said they didn't want me hanging with the PGs anymore. Sometimes I just don't feel like being with them anymore, but I am who am today because of them. I'll just feel like a dog with its tail between its legs if I went back to my old friends, and like I always remind my family, they weren't much of friends anyway so the change with being with the PGs now was the best thing that has happened to me. Sure, we're going through a very hard time right now, but this is when we have to stick together the most."

"I agree, Olive. I just wish Prima would've let one of us drive back. I admit that I'm still shaking by the way she was driving."

"It's okay now, Kitty. She scared the hell out of me as well as all of the other PGs. Ursula tried to act as if she wasn't, but I could tell she was and was even afraid to get on Prima about her driving. Prima has driven like that before when she's been mad about something."

"And I don't wanna be in the car again with her when she is mad, I'm saying that right now."

"Neither do I, Kitty, neither do I."

"So, have you tried to call Poppy?"

"Yeah, I have, but her phone goes to voicemail, and it's clear that a hell of a lot of people have been calling her and leaving messages because her voicemail is full. I asked the other PGs have they been trying to call her and they said they have as well. Have you?"

"No, not yet," I shamefully admitted. "I didn't wanna seem like I was bothering her. I know she still has some recovering to do, besides, I just knew all of you called her."

"Well, you're a part of the group so it would be nice for her to hear from you as well, I know she would appreciate it."

"Well, in that case then I will try and call her soon. I just hope she returns to school soon. The group isn't complete without her."

"You're right, it isn't. You can tell that someone is missing from it. It does seem weird how long she's been out of school, but she will be back and we will be one happy group once again."

I hope so, I thought. "Yeah, we will be."

CHAPTER 21

"Prima, your backyard is so beautiful!" I said in total admiration of her resort-style backyard that resembled a tropical paradise with a big, beautiful pool, palm trees, waterfalls, expensive-looking outdoor furniture and a spacious grill along with a bar for the adults. "It puts my backyard to shame."

"Well, thank you, Kitty," Prima said with a smile, as we all sat in these expensive chairs while enjoying grapefruit granitas that her mom made for us while we were at school. "But you shouldn't compare yourself to others. You live just fine like the rest of us."

I wish I had y'alls money, I thought. "Yeah, you're right, Prima."

"Well, I just wish Poppy's parents would stop their bullshit and let us see her. They know how long it's been," Ariana said.

The PGs nodded in agreement.

"Well, I'm not gonna stress myself out about it anymore. I don't know what the hell their problem is, either. We put together that beautiful vigil for her and have been trying to contact her every day and this is how they treat us? And I thought they were cool," Prima said, and ate some more of her granita.

"Me too," Rika said.

"Same here," Ursula said.

"Well, maybe they feel that she needs more time to recover. You know recovery goes in phases. She got out of the first phase of it by being in the hospital and now has been released, and now she's in the second phase of it by being at home. Maybe her parents don't want anyone interfering in the process, not even us," Lauren said.

"True, but them not letting us at least talk to her on the phone or whatever is just being selfish, I think," Prima said.

"Well, there's nothing we can do about it, she's their child. She doesn't belong to us," Olive said.

"She's a part of our group so her parents need to lighten up," Prima said.

"So, anyone excited about the Sahara Palms and Roses Festival in a few weeks?" Lauren asked, clearly trying to change the subject.

"Not really. Same shit different year," Prima honestly replied.

"I love it," Ariana said. "The beautiful horses, the flowers, the food, other entertainment."

"I love it because no other school has it," Rika said.

"Kitty, you should be excited about going to it since it's gonna be your first school event," Ursula said with a smile.

"Oh, I'm excited," I honestly replied. "But the newsletter said the female students have to wear a headpiece, and a fancy one."

"Yeah, it's like being at the Kentucky Derby, looks like it as well but with a bunch of teens. It's like a day prom but without the guys having to wear tuxedos and the girls having to wear formal dresses. We just have to wear day dresses but they have to be in good taste, or you can wear a skirt. The guys have to wear a day suit and a shirt with a collar, but a tie is optional," Prima said.

"It looks so fancy from last year's pictures and videos I've seen on the school's website," I replied. "But I really look forward to it."

"And since you're a part of this group, we always wear floral dresses —long or short—to this event. We've been attending it since freshman year. And your hat or headpiece has to be a solid color and match the main color of your dress—like for example, if you wear a white floral dress your hat or headpiece has to be white," Prima said.

"I got it," I replied with a smile. "I know you all are gonna be the belles of the ball."

"We always are!" Prima said with delight.

The PGs smiled and nodded in agreement.

Conceited much? But I did make a statement that would make Prima respond the way she did so I can't say that much, I thought.

Prima looked at her phone. "GIRLS!" she said as she jumped out of her seat so fast as if it was on fire.

"What, Prima?" the PGs asked in curiosity.

"They got them! They got those assholes who threw that red paint all over us when we walked out of the mall! They want us down at the station to see who they are!" Prima informed us.

We all gasped in shock!

"I didn't think they would ever catch them since they were completely covered where there was no way we were able to identify any of them," I said.

"I know, but they did! Let's go!" Prima said.

CHAPTER 22

"So, those are the random losers who threw all of that cheap red paint all over us as if it was blood, huh?" Prima said, as we all stood in a room and looked at the four suspects through a huge glass window—two boys and two girls—that were finally caught at least in this case, and I recognized one of them.

"They're probably from that cult that hates us," Ursula said.

"What cult?" Detective Markson asked.

The PGs looked at Ursula as if giving her a warning look not to say the "Kat Kult" since they didn't want anyone to know that's what they really called people who were pro-Kat and anti-PGs.

"Um, nothing. It's just that people do crazy shit to people all the time and they're usually a part of some kind of brainwashed group that tells them to do something and they do it. They just look like it," Ursula replied.

The PGs nodded in agreement.

"Do you all recognize any of them?" Markson asked.

"No, not at all," Prima said.

"I don't," Rika said.

"Never seen them," Ariana said.

"I can't say that I do," Lauren said.

"Neither can I," Olive said.

"I definitely don't," Ursula said.

"Kitty?" Markson said.

The PGs looked at me.

"Um, no, I don't know who any of them are," I lied. "I still consider myself new to the school and still don't know a lot of people so no, I have no idea."

"Very well," Markson said. "Since you all don't know who they are but they definitely know who all of you are, I will start from left to right. Sitting in the first seat is Thomas Reinhart; second seat is Valerie Bay; third seat is Chris Mentz; and in the last seat is Darlynn Foster."

"Don't have lunch with them."

That was her.

Darlynn Foster.

Now I knew her name because she sure as hell didn't tell me in the bathroom that day. Now it looked as if I should've been more afraid of her than she had me afraid of the PGs. It was clear that she was serious in not wanting me to have lunch with them that day, and maybe it was because her and her friends were planning this all along and didn't wanna include me in all of it since I had nothing to do with any of this. She knew what she was doing, and I felt she should suffer the consequences for it.

"We want to press full charges against all four of these losers," Prima said, obviously speaking for all of us.

"Yeah!" the PGs said in agreement.

"We're all still traumatized about it," Ursula said.

"That's right!" the PGs said in agreement about this as well.

I knew I was definitely still traumatized, but I had some relief now that they were all caught.

"What grade are they all in?" Rika asked.

"They're juniors like all of you," Markson replied. She looked at some papers she had in a folder. "Thomas and Valerie actually don't go to your school; they go to an online school. Chris just recently dropped out of Sahara Palms and hasn't been there since the first semester of his junior year, so the only one that still goes there is Darlynn."

The PGs nodded in agreement.

"Who turned them in?" Lauren asked.

"Valerie," Markson said.

We all shrieked in shock.

"She said they all got into a big fight over what they should do to all of you next. She said she already felt guilty enough about the first incident, and just didn't wanna have any part in the second one. They threatened her not to tell about the first one and she said she couldn't live with herself if she kept it a secret and that you all had the right to know it was them, so she said she was turning herself in and wanted the other three to come with her. When they refused, she came here by herself and told on them since everyone knew it was four people involved and not just one, and the rest of them confessed. She said she was not going down by herself, can't blame her for that," Markson said.

"And she shouldn't have. We want all the people involved in this to be punished for it and we got them," Ursula said.

"Exactly. And that Darlynn is gonna be sorry she ever walked the halls of Sahara Palms," Prima warned.

"Don't go making threats, Prima. Since this incident happened at the mall and not at school, you can still press charges against all of them, but there's not much the school can do about Darlene personally for what she was involved in outside of there. So I'm going to tell all of you right now that even though what'd happened to you all should not have happened, the best thing you can do is leave her alone," Markson suggested.

"Leave her alone? *Leave her alone*? What about us? No one has left us alone since Kat disappeared, and it's clear that they're not going to. I don't care what Markson says, if I see that bitch walking those halls at school then she's gonna regret she ever went to our school," Prima said.

We were all back over her house but were sitting in the family room.

"Look, we have to listen to what Markson says. We don't wanna get into any trouble, Prima. We already have a rep of being notorious, so if we hurt that girl then we're gonna be in trouble. *Big trouble*. We've already pressed charges against her and the others so that will be it until they go to trial. I want a full trial and I'm all set to testify. They caused all of us a lot of mental and emotional pain, stress, and trauma. I admit that I still get nightmares over it," Ariana said.

"I thought I was the only one," Lauren said.

"Yeah, me as well," Olive said.

"I still can't stop thinking about it, either," I said.

"Yeah, and it's all because those losers thought we had something to do with Kat's disappearance. We don't know where the hell that girl is. As far as I'm personally concerned, this could be a setup," Prima said.

The PGs looked at her. I found what she said very interesting.

"Why do you think it's a setup, Prima?" Rika asked.

"Because everyone is out to get us, that's why," Prima said. "They wish they were us and the ones that know they can't be us are trying to ruin us, that's why. Look what those losers did to us? Look at the threatening calls and texts we've been getting? Look what happened to our cars? I think they're behind those things, too, we just can't prove it and they didn't admit to doing it because they were asked. And this all started *before* we were splashed by those fuckers with that fake blood. People are trying to do everything they can to make us look guilty to everyone who loves us, that's what they're trying to do.

"I know you all see this and feel the way I do about it. But we can't let them win. And this is the start to them not winning now that they will be charged with this. You see how they all got into a fight and they said that Valerie chick threatened to tell on them all about doing it if they didn't come clean—at least she had a conscience. But there are gonna be others out there that are not gonna have the conscience that she has and are gonna try and hurt us even more. We got lucky this time, but the next time we might not be so lucky."

"Please don't talk like that, Prima. That scares me. I'm already scared enough and on edge about all of this," Lauren said.

"Me too," Olive said.

"Count me in," Rika said.

"But, girls, look what's happening now? They got the people who did this to us, and Poppy is out of the hospital and at home. Things are looking up," Ursula said.

"But we still don't know who hurt Poppy," Olive said.

"And don't forget we still don't know who vandalized our cars," Lauren said.

"Yeah," the PGs replied.

"I think it was those four who also did that shit to us even though they said they had nothing to do with it, they just don't want anymore charges against them. They look like some criminals. You see how Markson said they got in a big fight and Valerie snitched on all of them. I know she better watch her back in prison!" Prima said with a laugh.

"Yeah, maybe," Olive said. "But if they had something to do with our cars, wouldn't Valerie have snitched on that as well?"

The PGs looked at Prima.

"I would think that she would've, so yeah, you're right, it could've been different people. It was obviously different people since Markson did bring it up to them and they said they had nothing to do with it. Maybe they really didn't, but they did the red paint incident. Remember, girls, we have a hell of a lot of haters, more than we know, so I'm definitely not ruling out that it was a whole different group of Kat-Kult members who did it," Prima said.

"And neither are any of us. Right, girls?" Ursula said.

"Right," the PGs replied.

I stared at Olive since she just didn't seem to be sure about who attacked Poppy or who vandalized their cars, but since we found out who threw the red paint on us then we would find out who did all of the other things as well . . . I hoped.

THE POPULAR GIRLS
CAUGHT!
THE WHO-DONE-IT FAKE BLOOD SPLASH ATTACK
ON THE PGs HAS FINALLY BEEN SOLVED!
ONE CASE DOWN, THREE MORE TO GO!

Well, score one for the PGs!

The attackers in the case of the fake blood were finally caught when one of them caught the case of the guilts and couldn't take it anymore. And we couldn't blame Valerie Bay, a junior at an online school, for finally having a conscience and coming forward about what she'd done, but she didn't have the backing of her partners in crime, Thomas Rhinehart, a junior also at an online school; Chris Mentz, a Sahara Palms junior dropout; and Darlynn Foster, a Sahara Palms junior.

The PGs have pressed full charges against the four as they should've, but Prima was also in the room making threats that these four couldn't see or hear about how they were gonna be sorry they did this to them, and given Prima and the PGs' notorious ways, we would take the threat pretty seriously if we were these four. She especially made it to Darlynn since she's the only one who attends Sahara Palms, or we will soon be saying that she used to, because the school has yet to make a decision on what they want to do with her.

We also got in contact with Detective Jennifer Markson, who's been assigned to the cases involving the PGs, Kat Black, as well as PG Poppy, because we wanted to know about the PGs' cars being vandalized. She said they still didn't have any leads on it and that the four who did this assault on them said they had nothing to do with it.

And for some reason, we believe them.

The PGs have pissed off a lot of people throughout the years, and now it seems like people want to let them see how it feels to hurt people, and feel that they can take out their disdain for them by committing crimes against them, even though there is still no proof that they had anything to do with Kat's disappearance, but there's people, especially those four arrested today, who still believe they have everything to do with it.

Seems that even though one of these cases is solved, there are so many more to go, and we'll be on top of it all.

"I just don't ever see an end to any of this," I said in response to this latest post, and scrolled down to look at the thousands of comments. It was really unbelievable how seven girls could have so many people intrigued by them, and I was part of the group. I knew that most girls would kill to be with a popular group of girls, but if there was any time that they should see that it was not all what they thought it was, especially with the PGs, then the time was now.

I called Olive since I was worried about her.

"Kitty, hey. What's up?" she said.

"Hi, Olive. I just wanted to give you a call since you seemed so down at Prima's house once we got back from the police station."

"I was, Kitty. I'm a little better now. It's just that so much is happening and I just wanted this time to be a great time for all of us since we're juniors this year, but it's been nothing but hell for the past year since Kat disappeared. And then Prima has you come into all of this madness without even a thought about how you would feel about it. Has she even asked you how you felt about hanging with us?"

"Actually, she has during Gym. She just told me that this was not the experience that she wanted me to have while hanging with you all, but she said it was an experience that we were all going through together now and one that we would never forget. She said thirty years from now we will all be talking about what's going on right now and for the rest of our lives."

"Yeah, she's not lying about that. We have had much more of a dramatic All-American high school experience if you ask me. But I have to admit, nothing beats being a PG."

"It doesn't seem like it, because you all have a ton of people on your side all the time. People really believe that you all are innocent of everything that you've been accused of doing. I think more harm is being done to all of you and to me as well, but where are all of the people who claim they love us? How come no one is coming to our defense about any of this?"

"Because they're cowards, Kitty, but in reality, they really don't have to. People love to love us but do it from afar. And unfortunately, as you know by now, people love to hate us as well. We have people all over the world following us on social media and we haven't been active on there as much since Kat's disappearance because we didn't feel like going through all the deleting and blocking people for their nasty comments and other shit when they have no idea what the hell is going on; or having comments turned off completely because we do like to hear what the nice people say. I just don't wanna deal with any of it and especially since I wasn't with the PGs when Kat disappeared, and you especially don't need it since you had nothing to do with any of it. I just feel like we're going in circles and are never gonna break out of the cycle of all of this madness."

"I think we will, Olive. Look what happened today? I think if more people have a conscience like Valerie then these cases will get solved a lot faster."

"Yeah, I know they will, but there's more people who commit crimes that don't have a conscience than the ones who do. I have a feeling that was Valerie's first offense, even though Markson didn't tell us that."

"Yeah, I think it is, too, because she looked the most scared and upset out of all of them. And, Olive, before I forget, that's her."

"What? That's who?"

"Darlynn. She's the one who told me on the first day in the bathroom at Sahara Palms not to have lunch with you all. I just couldn't get myself to tell Markson the truth that I did recognize someone out of the four because I didn't know her name and I didn't want the PGs asking me a million questions."

She shrieked! "Are you serious, Kitty?"

"Yeah, I am. I instantly recognized her."

She let out a huge sigh. "Okay, thanks for letting me know, but I don't think Prima and the rest of the PGs should know, don't you agree?"

"Yeah, I agree, that's why I didn't say anything when I saw her because Prima has already threatened to cause Darlynn bodily harm if she's allowed back at school since she's the only one who goes there. Do you think Prima will make good on that?"

"If she doesn't get caught she will, or she will have someone who's so in love with her do it and there are a lot of people she could contact."

This sent chills through me.

"Well, I hope she doesn't do anything because the last thing we need is for one of us to get in serious trouble. We already have one of us who was beaten within an inch of her life, and we still have no idea who did it, so I think we should try and discourage Prima in every way possible not to hurt that girl. She's already been charged with what she did and we should just leave it at that."

"I think you're right, Kitty."

CHAPTER 23

I PULLED MY BOOKS OUT OF MY LOCKER FOR THE FIRST THREE periods when I received a call on my phone.

Blocked.

I didn't answer calls like these, so I continued to get my things for my classes. My phone finally stopped ringing . . . but rang again seconds later.

Blocked.

I sighed and decided to go against my own word and answer it.

"Hello?" I said with caution.

"Hi, Kitty."

It was Poppy!

"Poppy?!" I said in a whisper and I'd hoped she heard me since the halls were loud and wild like the way they always were every morning and especially afternoon.

"It's me," she confirmed.

"My God, Poppy! We've been trying for weeks and weeks to get in contact with you! What's going on? Are you okay?"

"No I'm not, Kitty."

I gasped in shock. I looked to my right down the hall and the PGs were up to their usual antics—some checking themselves out in their

Chanel mirrors, some taking selfies, some texting who knows who, and Prima being all over Jaxson. Yeah, typical day for the PGs, and it was good that they were able to carry on like this considering the fact what they'd gone through and what they were still going through.

"Um, what's wrong? I thought everything was fine with you. Are you back in the hospital?"

"No I'm not, Kitty. It's just that I need to talk."

I looked over at the PGs once again . . . and walked in the opposite direction early to class since I needed to get away from all of the deafening noise. "Have you contacted any of the other PGs?"

"No, I haven't."

It was something in her voice that just didn't sound right. She just didn't sound like the same Poppy that I knew when I first met her. But I felt this was all due to her traumatic experience and it was something that I knew she would never forget so I could see why she was so down about it and I knew she would be for a very long time.

I tried to make her feel better. "Are you looking forward to the Sahara Palms and Roses Festival?"

"I'm not going this year," she informed me.

I gasped once again in shock. "Why not?"

She sighed. "Kitty, you know what happened to me."

"And I'm sure you know what has happened to us since what'd happened to you. I don't mean to compare incidents but none of this has been good, Poppy, in fact, it's been pretty fucked up—excuse my language."

"I know it has, Kitty. You don't deserve all of this. Your timing was horrible to come here."

"Yeah, you can say that again and again, but it is what it is and at least I have friends."

Silence.

"Hello? Poppy?"

"I'm still here, Kitty."

"Hey, Kitty! Who are you talking to?" Rika said.

I didn't see Rika at all come up from behind me since we did walk together to our first-period class.

"It's—"

My phone accidentally lost the call, or at least that was what I wanted to believe.

"Just my mom," I lied. "She always wants to make sure I get to school okay and tells me to call her. I just forgot to do it this morning, so she called me like she always does when I forget."

She gave me a skeptical stare. "Okay, cool. Well, let's get to class so we're not late."

I suddenly felt lightheaded after just that brief conversation with Poppy, but I was determined to finish what we were talking about because it was clear she wanted to talk.

Just what the hell was going on?

I stared out the window of Darius' room.

"Kitty? What's wrong? You haven't been yourself all day today," he said as he watched me stare out of the window. "We don't have to study for the test this week if you don't want to."

I sighed as I stared at the overcast skies since it looked as if it was about to start raining. I turned towards him as he still sat at his desk. "I just have so much on my mind, Darius. I just feel like I'm in this whole new world since my family moved out here and I've been attending Sahara Palms. And never in a million years did I ever think I would be hanging with the PGs. But not everything is the way I thought it would be."

"Yeah, it definitely doesn't seem like it. I know some of the stuff you all have been through like everyone else knows, even though you had nothing to do with any of this. You truly just came in at a bad time, Kitty. Everything was already in motion once you started hanging with them, and it's clear that people have been messing with you, too. I'm sorry about that."

I smiled. "Thank you, Darius."

I sighed. I didn't know whether or not I wanted to tell him that I'd heard from Poppy today, and that was the first time I'd heard from her since she was badly beaten in the bathroom. I just couldn't get myself to tell Olive at all, much less the other PGs and especially Prima most of all. I believed her when she said she hadn't talked to any of them yet because one of them would've said if she had. I wanted to tell them so bad but had to convince myself to keep it to myself. But I felt that I had to tell someone.

"Kitty, you're kinda scaring me, girl. If you can see how you look I think you would scare yourself as well. I've never seen you look like this so please, tell me what's on your mind because it's obviously been on your mind all day. I noticed the way you looked in class today, and I wasn't sure if you even wanted to study after school and was surprised when you told me you still wanted to and that you would be here, and here you are. It's okay if you don't want to actually study, I understand. You know I'm always gonna listen to what people have to say because sometimes we need just need to talk, you know? It's not healthy to hold things in."

"I know," I replied.

"You can trust me, Kitty."

Can I really? I thought.

His trust was about to be put to the test.

"I talked to Poppy today. She called me," I informed him.

He looked confused. "Okay. Well, that doesn't seem like a big thing since I know she has called all of the other PGs to talk to them."

"No she hasn't," I informed him.

He gave me a shocked look. "Oh . . . *oh*. Well, why not? Did she say?"

"No, she hasn't. It was just something in her voice, Darius. She just didn't sound the same when I was talking to her. I know she's went through a traumatic experience and all, but why wouldn't she call all of the other PGs? I know they're always on the phone with different guys and mostly lurking on social media for right now, but I know that if she did call them they would've told me. Maybe she just couldn't get through to any of them so she called me, and is just saying that she hasn't called any of them. I honestly don't know what to think. I guess I'm still surprised to hear from her."

"Have you talked to her since getting cut off from her since earlier today?"

"No, I haven't."

"Do you wanna call her right now?"

I stared at him. I really wanted to, but I really wanted to be alone if I did.

"I'll be quiet. I promise," he said.

I took a deep breath. "Okay." I got out my phone and called Poppy since I hadn't heard from her since this morning.

Her phone rang.

And rang.

And rang.

It rang a few more times before I decided to hang up.

"Either she doesn't have her phone anywhere near her or she sees that it's me and doesn't wanna talk. I hope it's not the latter."

"I hope not either."

As I sat at home still trying to concentrate on my homework and on the test I had in American Government this week that I didn't study with Darius at his house for, I just couldn't get it off of my mind that I actually heard from her and that she didn't call any of the other PGs. She called me, I didn't call her. She sounded depressed and still upset and she had every right to sound and be that way. But we got disconnected when Rika came up to me, so I never got to finish the conversation we'd started.

My phone rang.

It was Poppy!

"Hello? Poppy?" I said.

"Yeah, it's me. Hey," she said in a somber tone.

"Did you see that I tried to call you back earlier when I was over Darius' house studying? I didn't get an answer from you."

"I was having therapy, Kitty. I can't have my phone with me while I do."

"Therapy? You mean physical therapy?"

"No, mental and emotional therapy."

"I understand."

We sat in silence for a few seconds.

"Well, I'm glad you called me earlier today. Have you talked to the other PGs yet?"

"No, I haven't."

Something about this gave me a weird feeling.

"How come?"

"I just wanna talk to you for right now. Is that okay?"

"Sure, that's okay. Do you want me to tell them that I spoke to you?"

"No," she didn't hesitate to say.

Just what the hell was going on?

I wanted to ask her why not, but she had her reasons. "Um, Poppy. The PGs and I had a beautiful vigil at school hoping and praying that you would get better and you have. Your parents haven't allowed any of us to see you, and I have to tell you that the PGs are really mad about that. We even tried to visit you at your house when you were released from the hospital and the security guard at the front entrance to the community you live in said we weren't on the list of approved visitors to see you and we weren't on the list of approved visitors at the hospital as well. Why weren't we? Prima and the rest of the PGs have really been mad about this and Prima was driving all recklessly coming from your house and ran a red light and we were pulled over by a cop and everything. The way she was driving scared the fuckin' shit out of me—excuse my language."

"That's the PGs for you. They're not known for being notorious for nothing."

"Poppy, you talk like you're not friends with them anymore."

"Kitty, I've been through a harrowing ordeal, okay? I almost didn't survive. No one can tell me who did this to me and I'm really pissed off about it. It didn't happen to any of them, this happened to me."

"I know, Poppy, but me and the rest of the PGs really wanna be here for you. We're all friends, but your parents are acting as if we're your enemies."

"They're just being parents. This has been just as hard for them as it's been for me and they don't want all of the PGs fuckin' drama brought around me right now. They brought all of this shit on themselves and they know it, and they dragged you into it. I feel sorry for you, Kitty. You had no idea what you were getting into when Prima let you into the group, and everyone knew it, they just didn't say anything."

"Well, I believed Prima when she told me that she wanted me to have the ultimate All-American high school experience and there was no better group to be in than the PGs."

"Yeah, well, now you know that things aren't as great and wonderful being a PG. And I hate to say it, but I have a feeling that things are gonna get way worse before they get better."

"My goodness I hope not, Poppy. I feel like I'm already in too deep with all of this, and I haven't done anything to anyone."

"I know you haven't, Kitty. You're truly the most innocent one in all of this. I honestly wish you had the chance to find other friends and you wouldn't be in all of this drama."

Yeah, sometimes I wish that, too, I thought. "Well, I'm with you all so I'm staying with you all."

She let out a sigh.

"What?"

"Nothing, Kitty. I wish I can talk to you longer, but I need to rest up before dinner. I'll try and talk to you tomorrow."

"Okay, Poppy. Take care."

"Bye, Kitty."

I continued to sit at my desk as I stared at my closed books. There was no way I could do any homework right now. Something about the conversation gave me strange vibes; it was truly unexplainable. I felt as if she wanted to tell me something but just didn't know if she could trust me in keeping it a secret, even though she said that she could trust me. But I was glad she told me the reason why her parents didn't want her to see us and I could definitely understand it because we had a lot of drama going on in the group and that was the last thing she needed was us to be bitchin' and complaining and whining to our friend who clearly had suffered a very harrowing ordeal physically and mentally and was going to therapy for it.

We may have been through some ordeals ourselves, but nothing like the one she'd been through.

I couldn't take it. I had to call Olive.

"Kitty, hi. You called right on time. I just got done studying. So, what's up?"

"Um . . . ." I paused.

I just didn't know if I should've told her that I'd spoken to Poppy earlier today at school before classes started, and now again just a few minutes ago. There was a reason why Poppy wanted to talk to me and not the rest of them right now, and only she knew why, but I believed it was because she didn't feel like hearing all of the drama, and I couldn't blame her if that was true. But then I thought about the fact that Poppy never told me not to tell them that I'd talked to her.

"Hello? Kitty?"

"Yeah, I'm still here. Um . . . ." *Just say it,* I thought. "Um, I have to tell you something, but you have to promise me that you won't tell the other PGs or anyone, and I'm serious."

"Wow, okay. You know you have my trust, Kitty. What is it?"

"I . . . I spoke to Poppy today."

"WHAT?!" she shouted.

"Yes, Olive. I spoke to her today. She actually called me first before first-period classes, and I lost the call while going to class. I tried her again while I was over Darius' house, but didn't get an answer. Then, she called me just a few minutes ago."

"Well, this is interesting because it's clear that she hasn't called any of us at all since she's been out of the hospital and back home. If she can call you then she can call any of us. All of us has tried to call her several times and we either get no answer or it just goes to her voice-mail and we do leave messages. Her voicemail actually became full— but she called *you*? Did she say why she hasn't answered or returned any of our calls or why she hasn't called any of us at all?"

"No, she hasn't told me why, Olive. But she doesn't sound like the same person. I don't like the vibes I'm getting from her now."

"What do you mean?"

I sighed. "I don't know really. She just sounds different. Her voice sounds different and everything, but I just think it's all of the stress and trauma that she's been through. She sounds severely depressed."

"Yeah, I can believe that. You're right, just by what you've told me, she doesn't sound like the Poppy we all know. I'm glad you decided to tell me that you've spoken to her, Kitty. I just can't believe she's acting as if she doesn't wanna talk to any of us, though. She's acting as if we're her enemies, and her parents are just being jerks."

"Well, she told me why we all weren't able to come visit her at the hospital and now at her home."

"And why is that?"

"Because they don't want us spewing all of this drama on her. It's clear that she knows what's been happening to us since her incident, and her parents just want her to be able to recover in peace without all of the drama that you have to admit the PGs would've been causing while we were there."

She chuckled. "Yeah, I can't lie. You're right about that, Kitty. So, I guess I can't get upset about her parents now being that way because my parents would've been that way as well; I think all our parents would be. They actually still don't a hundred percent approve of me being with the PGs because they think they're too notorious to be around, and now they really think it."

"Well, if I felt that way then I would've just left the group to find other friends, but you all are the only ones who befriended me on my first day. No one else gave a shit that I was the new girl."

She chuckled once more. "Yeah, we had to put ourselves in your place, Kitty. It can be very lonely being the new girl so I'm glad you've stuck with us because no one has been tested more than you have at your new school when it comes to you hanging with us."

"Yeah, you're right, Olive. This has gone far beyond what I have expected when I came out here, but hey, that's life. I believe that things will get better as soon as all of these other cases are solved, especially about Poppy."

"So, you did ask her who did that to her?"

"Yeah, I did. She said no one could tell her who did it to her because she says she doesn't remember and wanted to see if anyone knew who did it to her—but how could she not remember? She was attacked in the bathroom at school, or maybe she really doesn't know who did it. Hopefully, her memory will come back about it soon. I just don't want her to get hurt like that again."

"Yeah, none of us do. Did you ask her about the festival that's coming up?"

"Yeah, and she told me she wasn't going this year."

"Well, I'm not surprised, but she needs to let all of us know that, not just you. I won't say anything for right now, but she has to tell us herself if she's going or not."

"Well, by that time I'm sure she will."

"Is there anything else she told you, Kitty?"

"Like what?"

"Like, anything."

I didn't know what it was that she wanted me to tell her. "No, she didn't tell me anything else of importance, only that she is seeing a therapist because of what'd happened to her, and like I said, she didn't sound like herself, but I believe that's only natural for right now."

"Yeah, I believe it is as well. Anyone who went through what she went through won't really sound the same and that can be for some time so don't expect for her to be the same person when she returns to school. But you know we all gotta be there for her since she's a PG."

"Yeah, I know, Olive. I'm definitely gonna be there for her like all the rest of you because like all the rest of you, Poppy is my friend and I just wanna find out just as much as anyone who the hell did that to her because I'm still scared, Olive, that any one of us could be next."

"I know, Kitty. It's very possible that one of us could be. That's why we always need to stay vigilant and be with one another whenever possible. I mean, what happened to Poppy happened in the school bathroom obviously very early in the morning because unlike all of us, she's one of those very early risers, as they call them. She's usually the first to get to school out of all of the students here and especially us. So yeah, I believe the person who did this to her knew all of this as well and that's why they attacked her when they did."

"I haven't been able to go back in that bathroom since. This is crazy. I'm just happy that at least she's getting better and I did hear from her. I just wish she was going to the festival because it'll be my first one and I would love to have all of the PGs there."

"Well, you never know, Kitty. Maybe she'll be a little better by then and change her mind."

"I sure hope so."

CHAPTER 24

festival that's coming up?" Mom asked me as she put a plate of pancakes and bacon in front of me.

"Yeah, I have a lot of ideas, but they're all too expensive. This is one of the fanciest events besides prom which is next year when I'm a senior. I just wanna fit in with the PGs. I already know that they're gonna look like some premier designer models with big, fancy hats on there."

"A high school Kentucky Derby, huh? Never heard of it. This must be unique to Sahara Palms," Dad said, and then sipped his coffee as he looked at his phone.

"It is, Dad, but it's not exactly like the Kentucky Derby. But it's gonna be my first-ever school event there and I wanna look just as nice as I know the PGs are gonna look. They've been to all of them since freshman year and told me that they always wear floral dresses and hats that match the main color of their dresses."

"Wow," Mom said as she sat down. "I guess you better find a look and find one fast. You know we'll pay for it, but don't get too crazy. Just pick out a dress, hat, and shoes, and we'll see what we can do."

"I already have something picked out," I said with excitement.

"That was painless," Mom said, and then sipped her coffee.

"Well, I hope the cost of all the items are as painless well," Dad said.

We all laughed.

I walked into my bedroom after coming home from a drama-free day at school, and gasped to what I saw lying on my bed.

A beautiful Coach silk V-neck long floral A-line dress in a beautiful magenta color with multicolored flowers on it; a pair of Coach Aubree sandals with a kitten heel that I was gonna have to practice walking in because I didn't wear heels at all, and a big, beautiful magenta hat.

"Like it?" Mom asked.

"Oh, Mom! I love it! Thank you!"

We hugged.

"Now you'll fit in with your friends. The dress and shoes were actually 30% off so the time couldn't be more perfect for me to pick it up earlier today. I'm glad they had your size in the dress and shoes. The hat was less than $100."

I tried everything on. "How do I look?"

"Beautiful. Like I said, you're gonna fit right in with your friends."

"I hope so." I sat on my bed with my whole look on.

She sat right next to me. "Something wrong?"

I shrugged. "I feel so beautiful in this outfit, but I just don't know how this event is gonna go. It just seems like everywhere we go, people always seem to be out to hurt us."

"Well, they caught the people who threw the paint on you all, so you don't have to worry about them."

"Yeah, but they haven't caught the people who vandalized the PGs' cars, or who hurt Poppy. And we *still* don't know what happened to Kat Black."

"I know, honey, but all of these things will be solved. Nothing stays a secret forever. I just want you to be able to have a great time at this event and try to forget about all of these bad things that has happened."

"Yeah, and that's exactly what I want to do." I looked around. "Oh, no!"

"What is it?"

"I don't have a purse to match my outfit!" I said in a panic.

"Relax, Kitty. I'll be right back."

Several minutes later, she returned with a purse in a Coach dustcover. She gave it me.

I gasped as I pulled out one of her very expensive bags. A Coach Tabby 26 bag in beautiful genuine alligator in a violet pink color with a pewter-colored C in the middle. "Mom, oh, my God! You're gonna let me carry *this* bag? You've only carried it once!"

"It's a special occasion, sweetie, and it looks beautiful with your dress. Now you guard it with your life, understand?"

"Of course, Mom. And it looks like it came with my dress! So beautiful! Now I really feel like I'm gonna fit in with the PGs!"

"Glad to hear it."

I stood up once again and looked in my full-length mirror at my completed outfit. I was really looking forward to this and was hoping we would have a great time, but if not, I knew my outfit looked great!

CHAPTER 25

"HEY, PGS! THE MOST BEAUTIFUL GIRLS AT SAHARA PALMS AND ALL the other schools! Look this way for us so we can get some pictures of you all!" a photographer yelled out to us.

Have you seen all the girls at all of the other schools? I thought, but smiled big regardless.

It was a beautiful and bright sunny day, and the temperature was perfect in the low 80s, which felt like summer to me where I'm from. And I was glad that the weather cooperated since this whole event was outside. We stood with our floral dresses on with beautiful shoes and purses, and just as I expected, all of the PGs looked like premier designer models and had on premier designer dresses to match, with Prima, Ursula, and Rika in Oscar de la Renta, Lauren in Dolce & Gabbana, and Ariana in Marchesa. Olive opted for a contemporary designer dress and wore a beautiful Alice + Olivia Becca embroidered black floral dress, a dress that was coincidentally on my wish list on a website. They all wore beautiful, eye-catching hats in a solid color that complemented their dresses as well as luxury shoes. I felt that I fit right in with my Coach look on, and was glad I'd chosen this look.

"PG Kitty, how do you feel about being at your first Sahara Palms event?" a random guy asked me, that I assumed to be working for the school newsletter or even yearbook, but then again, I didn't know.

"I feel great. I love the atmosphere, everyone looks beautiful, and I hope to have a lot of fun which I know I will. Thank you," I replied with a big smile.

"Thank you, PGs! Can we get each one of you individually?" another photographer asked.

"Sure!" Prima said, and we all stepped out of the way to let her have her shine.

"Do they always do this?" I asked Olive, as we watched cameras light Prima up in her beautiful dress and hat.

"Yeah, they do," she replied. "And did you know Prima's dress is over $5,000?!"

"Holy shit!" I said, but wasn't surprised. "It's downright stunning. All of our looks are on point."

"Yeah, and that's the whole point," Olive replied. "Ursula told me that Prima told her that her dad cussed her mom out for buying her a dress that expensive, because her mom is always buying all of these expensive clothes for herself."

"Well, like mother, like daughter!"

We laughed as we nodded in agreement.

Minutes later, after all of the PGs before me, it was my turn to take my individual pictures for everyone.

"Work it, Kitty!" Prima yelled out to me.

I smiled as cameras flashed on me, but didn't wanna have anything to do with "working it" and putting myself in provocative poses for pictures—not my thing. And I knew I was only getting this much shine because of the PGs. But I couldn't help to be upset that Poppy was not here enjoying all of this with us, as it was clear she meant what she said when she told me she wasn't going this year.

"Thank you, Kitty!" the photographers said.

"You're welcome," I replied with a smile.

Finally, we all walked into the event.

"Um, I meant to ask you, did Poppy tell you all she wasn't coming today?" I asked Olive.

"Nope," she replied. "And Prima's not showing it, but she's really pissed off that she didn't at least call one of us and tell us and we all did try to call her many times—but remember, none of them still know but me what you told me about her calling you."

"Thank you, Olive. I knew I could trust you not to tell."

We all went over to the Laduree macarons, and they looked delicious.

"Kitty, this is always our first stop here. The macarons. As you see, they look so beautiful and colorful that you don't know if you should eat them or just take a picture of them," Prima said.

"I'll do both," I replied, and took a few macarons and put them on my plate.

The PGs laughed in agreement and followed suit.

We also got tea poured for us in beautiful Herend teacups, and walked over to a pre-assigned table to wait for the horse race to start. I felt like I was in a whole different world now because I knew I was, and despite all that had happened since being with the PGs, I thought this moment was special and was honored to be attending my first school event with them.

"So, who's excited for the after-party out at Lake Mead tonight?" Ursula asked.

"Of course, as always!" Prima said, and ate one of her macarons.

"It's always lit, Kitty. You're gonna have a lot of fun. It's Sahara Palms tradition to go to Lake Mead for the after-party after this event. And as you will see, it's much more fun than this uppity event," Ariana said.

The PGs laughed and nodded in agreement.

"I really look forward to it," I said with a smile, but I was really taking in this moment right now. Like Ariana said, it was uppity, no doubt, but I'd never been to anything like it so I didn't mind at all and I was so far having fun, but it was clear that there was more fun that awaited us at the after-party later on.

CHAPTER 26

"Yeah, this after-party is lit like you said, Ariana," I said with a big smile as we walked down to the after-party at Lake Mead, and it was packed with Sahara Palms students with all of us still in our festival clothes. "Since we're at a lake, I thought I would have to go home and change first."

She laughed. "Oh, no, Kitty! The whole point is to wear here what we wore to the event."

"But everyone looks so nice. I would think everyone would be afraid to ruin their outfits."

"They don't care, Kitty. A lot of them have so much money that what they're wearing tonight would be the only time they wear it, especially for the PGs," she replied.

"I wish I could say the same," I said.

And I meant that. I didn't wanna ruin the most expensive dress I'd ever had because unlike the PGs, I didn't have it like them that I could wear $5,000 dresses only once and didn't care about getting them ruined after a wild after-party.

I smiled and bobbed my head to the catchy music, and it was a party indeed. People were dancing, smoking, drinking, live-streaming, taking pictures—doing everything that people at parties do. I laughed at Jaxson as he scooped up Prima as she screamed while he had her hat on and pretended as if he was gonna drop her in the water.

"He wouldn't dare do that!" Olive said with a laugh.

"I hope not!" I replied with a laugh as well.

"MY DRESS WAS $5,596!" Prima yelled as he dangled her while standing in the shallow part of the water.

"MY SUIT WAS OVER $2,000!" he mocked her with a laugh.

Olive and I looked at each other.

"So arrogant," she said with an eye roll. "They would have to yell that out for everyone to hear, and Prima would have to say the exact amount of hers. My dress was $975, but I guess it's not expensive enough to yell out to everyone."

"Mine was $595 but with 30% off so it was a lot less," I replied. "Sometimes I feel so poor around all of you."

"Not everyone is super rich that goes to our school, Kitty, so it's okay. I'm definitely not one of them."

"And I'm definitely, *definitely* not one of them," I replied with a grin. We laughed.

I smiled as I looked around some more as Rika talked to the same guy she was talking to at Brennen's party, while Lauren danced with the captain of the basketball team, as I was told by Olive. Ariana and Ursula were having drinks with male friends as well, and the guys were all wearing their hats, in fact, half of the guys here were wearing the girls' hats.

"The guys look funny wearing the girls' hats," I said.

She laughed. "Yeah, that's a tradition as well at this party for the guys to wear the girls' hats. But I love the way mine looks with my dress so I'm keeping mine on. Plus, guys are so reckless with their play fighting with each other I don't want mine ruined."

"Neither do I, especially since I didn't pay for it," I replied, but secretly wanted a guy to wear mine so it would look like I fit in.

But it was still very bright and sunny out here, and I was having a great time, and I still adhered to my parents' rules about what I shouldn't do at parties, and I was the only one who apparently was. Even Olive was now out by the shore dancing with a guy with a drink in her hand, but I wasn't the one to tell them what to do.

My phone rang.

It was Poppy!

"Hey, Poppy. How are you?"

"I'm okay, Kitty. I see all over social media and on people's live streams as I speak that you all are at the after-party now."

"Yeah, we are, Poppy," I confirmed.

"I'm not interrupting you in the middle of anything, am I?"

I wish, I thought. "No, you're not. I'm just standing around watching everyone else have fun, but I don't mind because it keeps me out of trouble."

"Yeah, that's true, Kitty. You wanna stay out as much trouble as you can because the PGs are in enough of it."

I almost dropped my phone. "Oh, my God, Poppy! What do you mean by that?"

"Well, you know how much trouble they're still in over all of the things that have been going on, Kitty, and people are getting their revenge on them for it. I just want you to stay out of it as much as possible."

"Oh, I will, Poppy. I don't go looking for trouble, and I feel that since I'm with the PGs, their troubles are mine."

"You had nothing to do with anything, Kitty, so please don't think that and please especially don't have them making you think that just because you hang with them now their troubles are now yours, too. I would still try and find other friends if I were you."

There was a reason why she was saying this, and I was determined to find out why. I also couldn't help but to think about the fact that she said *them,* when she talked about people getting their revenge on the PGs, but someone obviously got separate revenge on her.

"So, did you have fun at your first festival?" she asked.

"Yeah, I did. It was the best time I've had since I've been at the school. Everything and everyone was so beautiful. I can only imagine how prom is gonna be next year."

"Yeah, prom at Sahara Palms is out of this world. It's only the seniors, of course, so even if a girl or a guy doesn't have a date, they still go because it's not to be missed."

"Wow, I can't wait even though I know it's a year away."

"It's gonna come up fast," she said with no excitement in the tone of her voice.

Darius approached me while holding his phone in front of him. "Hey, PG Kitty! I'm livestreaming this event right now."

"Oh, my God! I've never been on anyone's livestream," I informed him.

"Well, you're on mine now! I have the most popular one in the school!" he excitedly informed me. "Who are you talking to?"

"Hello?" I said.

The call went dead once again.

"My mom," I lied with embarrassment. "I lost the call."

"Well, say hi to everyone, PG Kitty."

I looked right into his phone. "Hi," I said with a smile.

"Yeah, PG Kitty is out here looking all beautiful with her Coach dress and shoes and purse and matching pink hat. We all look lit today because we're Sahara Palms students, so we do it better than anyone. No other school has the kind of events we have!"

"And I'm glad to be a part of it," I replied with a smile.

"Glad to hear it, PG Kitty," he said. "Oh, shit, there's PG Lauren, the most beautiful girl in the whole school. I'll be back later, y'all."

I looked at him. "Why did you end it?"

"Because I can't concentrate when I see Lauren. She's just too beautiful for words."

"She really is. But talk to her, Darius. Here's your chance."

"Yeah, but she's already got Tremaine Talbot wearing her hat, which means she's not gonna give it to me to wear. He's the captain of the basketball team. Can't compete with tall, dark, athletic, and nice looking, and he takes a good education seriously most of all."

"But he's not her boyfriend, Darius," I said, trying to encourage him.

"Well, he might as well be," he replied as he still kept his phone pointed at her as she talked to Ursula and Prima.

Minutes later, Olive and I talked once again, and she was serious about not letting any guy wear her hat.

"I talked to Poppy again," I informed her.

"You did?!" she asked.

"Yeah, I did," I confirmed.

She shook her head with a smirk. "So, what did she want to tell you now that she acts like she can't tell the rest of us?"

I could see that Olive was really taking it personal that Poppy hadn't called her or any of the other PGs yet, and I couldn't say that I blamed her. But she had her reasons, and that's what I wanted to find out most of all.

"Well, she just wanted to know how I liked my first school event."

"If she was here she would've been able to see it for herself instead of having to call you and ask you about it or watch everyone's videos or livestreams of it," she replied with an eye roll and then sipped some more of her drink.

Yeah, she's mad, I thought. "Well, I told her that I had a lot of fun, but this after-party is more fun like how everyone said it would be. I wish she was here as well."

"And I think she was well enough to go to both the event and to come here. Sorry if I sound bitchy, but I just don't like the way she's acting towards all of us. We're her friends and this is not how you treat friends. You don't treat them like your enemies just because you went through a harrowing ordeal by yourself. We suffered right along with her."

But none of you were beaten within an inch of your life, I thought. "Yeah, we have. She obviously still needs time to heal physically, mentally, and emotionally, Olive, so I think we all need to respect that and give her that time."

"Yeah, I agree, but my thing is that she can call *you* and talk to *you,* but she can't call any of us?"

"I know, Olive. I wish she would call you all, I do. But I can't make her do anything."

"Yeah, I know, Kitty, you can't."

Lauren approached us. "Hey, girls."

"Hey," we replied with a smile.

"So, Kitty, are enjoying this after-party?" Lauren asked.

"Yes, I am, very much," I replied with a smile. *But not as much as I would like since no guy has asked me to dance or wear my hat or anything,* I thought.

"Yeah, this after-party is what we're all really waiting for when we're at the event," Lauren said, and then sipped her drink.

Suddenly, we heard screaming from the other PGs as well as other girls, and we looked in the direction of them and saw Jaxson and Darius, as well as Brennen and a few other guys, taking off their clothes!

"Oh, my God! What are they doing?" I asked as I turned away from looking at them.

"They're ready to jump in the water, Kitty!" Lauren said with a laugh. "They do this every year."

"Oh, my God! Is it okay to look?" I asked as I still turned away. "Did they take off *everything?*"

"No, they still have their boxer shorts on," Olive laughed.

I looked and saw all of them slapping hands with each other, and then ran out to the water and dove in. I started to laugh, especially at Darius. "You know Darius is doing this to impress you, Lauren, you know that, right?"

She laughed shyly. "Well, I'm impressed because I don't wanna get in that water even with a full swimsuit on!"

"Neither do I!" Olive said.

We all laughed.

The rest of the PGs came over to us.

"Those guys are crazy! I don't like being in big bodies of water that's not in a swimming pool, but that's just me," Prima said, as she was wearing her hat again.

"Well, Darius and Brennen are on the swim team so they're used to swimming in any and everything," Ariana said.

"Still seems so unsafe and all," Ursula said. "They go out so far and you just don't know how deep it really is."

"Or if you'll get tangled up in anything down there. That's what scares me about getting in there," Lauren said.

The PGs nodded in agreement.

Suddenly, all of the guys popped up out of the water and swam back to shore as fast as they could. They ran to the shore as we all stared at them in curiosity.

"We need to call 911," Jaxson said. "There's a car down there."

CHAPTER 27

WE ALL STOOD HELPLESSLY BY WHILE WE WATCHED THE CAR GET towed out of the water and on to the shore as people took pictures and videos, and Darius live-streamed it while now fully dressed once again. The cops stood a few feet in front of us so we wouldn't interfere with the process. From what I'd seen, no one had left the party, and there were even more curious spectators here.

The car, small in size, was covered in all kinds of debris and it was hard to tell what make, model, and color it was, and we watched it as it was put on a flatbed truck, dripping with debris and water.

"How the hell did a car get down there?" Olive said.

"It happens," I replied.

"Yeah, y'all are all seeing this live just as we all are," Darius said as his hand shook while he had his phone out in front of him but had it pointing to the car. "The guys and I just went for the traditional after-party swim and played our game about how low could we go, and we went pretty low in the water but then saw the top of the car. We knew what it was, y'all. Damn, this is fucked up. I hope no one is in there because we can't see whether or not there is because the windows are darkly tinted."

"Is anyone in there?" Jaxson asked any cop.

"We're not allowed to say whether or not there is," a cop replied to him.

I felt my heart in my throat. I couldn't believe I was standing by witnessing all of this. I'd never seen anything like this before in my life. I looked up to the sky and clouds started to roll in. "That doesn't sound good," I said to Olive.

"It doesn't," she said.

My phone rang.

It was Poppy!

"Hello?" I said, as if I didn't know it was her. I began to walk away from the PGs.

"It's me," she said with a sigh. "I'm watching Darius' live stream right now. Do they have any idea whose car that is?"

I looked back at all of the PGs as they all stared back at me. I felt a rippling wave of chills all throughout my body. Here I was talking to Poppy, and none of them knew it except Olive that I had been back in contact with her in the past few days including today, and she still had yet to talk to any of them. "No, they haven't said. As you see since you're watching it right now, it's hard to even make out what kind color it is because there's so much nasty debris all over it. It looks like it's been down there for a while."

"Yeah, it probably was."

"Hey, Kitty," Prima said as all of the rest of the PGs surrounded me.

I dropped my phone out of being startled. "Hey," I said, as I picked up my phone. I saw that I'd lost the call once again.

"Who were you talking to?" Prima asked.

"My dad," I lied. "Him and my mom wanted to know what time I would be home since they think for some reason I've been out long enough even though it's still daylight. I thought they were calling me about this but it's clear that they haven't seen or heard about it yet."

Olive gave me a look of pure skepticism, and she had every right to do that because she knew I was lying my ass off and I was.

"Well, it looks like the party is over," Ariana said, as we still watched the debris-covered car on the flatbed truck as cops surrounded it and talked to each other.

"Yeah, that pretty much goes without saying," Ursula said. "And damn, I was having so much fun!"

"Tell me about it," Prima said.

"Well, think about it, girls. If it wasn't for the guys' discovery then that car would've sat down there for who knows how much longer," Lauren said.

"It looks like it's been down there for a very long time," Rika said. "Eeeewwww! All that debris all over it! Gross!"

The PGs nodded in agreement.

Several more minutes went by, and we watched as the cops questioned Darius, Jaxson, Brennen, and all of the rest of the guys who made the discovery.

I still couldn't believe I was standing out here witnessing all of this, and we were all having so much fun. Never did I think something like this was going to happen here. I was hoping that we could have a drama-free after-party, but it was not to be.

Suddenly, we heard screaming coming from the parking lot. We all looked in that direction, and saw Zoe running down to the lake with what it looked like her friends and parents!

"OH, MY GOD! NO! OH, MY GOD!" Zoe said as she cried. "LET ME SEE THE LICENSE PLATE! LET ME FUCKIN' SEE IT!"

One of the cops tried to console her while another one put on a pair of gloves and removed some of the debris off the back-license plate:

KB SPHS

Kat Black Sahara Palms High School.

Zoe screamed as she collapsed to the ground as her family and friends tried to help her to her feet.

It was confirmed to be Kat Black's car.

CHAPTER 28

"Kitty, we're so sorry, honey. We know how much of a great time you were having at the event and even at the after-party, that's why we didn't wanna bother you while you were there," Mom said, as we sat at the kitchen table talking.

"I know, Mom. We were having so much fun there . . . until the guys decided to take a swim and the PGs told me that's a tradition for them—but now look what happened? What if they didn't take that swim? Kat's car would still be down there," I said, as I wiped tears from my eyes. I took another sip of my mom's hot chocolate, a favorite of mine and something that she always made for me when she wanted to lift my spirits. "I feel so connected to her case, Mom. And it was just so surreal when they pulled her car out of the water, but I had no idea it was her car because no one talked about her car or anything. Gosh, it was down there for over a year now. I feel so bad for her family."

"We all do, honey."

"And we still don't know if Kat was in the car or not," I said.

"She was," Dad confirmed as he walked into the kitchen with his phone in his hands. "I just got off the phone with Gus, Kat's dad. Her body was so badly decomposed that they only knew it was her because of the car, license plate, as well as her purse and ID that was still in pretty good condition and that was incredible because the inside of the car was full of water." He sighed. "No parent should have to go through this."

"You're right, no parent should," Mom said. "This is why we stay on you, Kitty. I know you get annoyed by it, but it's what we have to do."

"I know, and now I see why. But I don't understand how she ended up driving into the water. What the hell?"

"Well, that's what we're all gonna find out. Have your friends talked about this?" Dad asked.

I sighed. "Well, they told me they had nothing to do with it and if she was in her car under water then what did they have to do with it? It's clear she drove herself to wherever she was going to or coming from and obviously got sidetracked about something. It can happen to anyone."

"Exactly right, Kitty. But all of your friends and everyone needs to be questioned once again now that her car and body have been found," Dad said.

"I agree, Dad," I said.

"Including you," Dad said.

"What?!" I said with shock. "Why me?"

"Because I'm sure your friends as well as other people have been talking about this to you, Kitty, so you need to tell the cops everything that they have told you about this case. Kat has been found and if there was foul play involved in this, then there's gonna be a lot of trouble no one is gonna be prepared for," he informed me.

My mom gave me the same look as Dad.

I was scared to death because he was right.

Hours later, upstairs in the privacy of my room, I looked at the PG site:

THE POPULAR GIRLS
SAHARA PALMS HIGH SCHOOL STUDENT KAT
BLACK'S CAR AND BODY HAVE BEEN FOUND

And on all days at that. As everyone knows, Sahara Palms High School had their annual Sahara Palms and Roses Festival, and things went as they normally did. But what happened at the traditional after-party at Lake Mead was anything but traditional.

A group of guys went for their show-off swim, as we call it, because we know they do it to impress the girls, but when they came up out of the water, something was wrong because according to witnesses, they looked terrified. They informed everyone that there was a car underneath the water . . . and there was.

And it was Kat Black's car along with her body inside of it.

She had been down there since the day she went missing which was a little over a year ago, and the car was identified as being hers by her vanity back-license plate, KB SPHS—Kat Black Sahara Palms High School—by her sister Zoe, who screamed and really made a scene, and no one stopped her from her grief.

Why are we talking about this on this PG blog? Well, it's because for over a year and still now, the PGs have been suspected of having something to do with Kat's disappearance, but now that she has been found, will any of them come clean now if they had something to do with how her and her car ended up in the lake? There is still no proof that the PGs had any involvement in this, but hopefully now we will get some answers because we can't believe that no one knows absolutely nothing.

R.I.P., Katerina "Kat" Black.

Tears streamed from my eyes. "Yeah, someone knows something, and I'm not gonna rest until I find out everything. I don't want my friends accused of something they say they didn't do. Why would they lie to me?" I said, as if someone was in my room with me.

My phone rang.

Poppy!

"Hey, Poppy."

"Hey, Kitty. Sounds like you've been crying. Are you okay?"

"Yeah, I have been crying but I'll be okay. I was just crying about Kat."

"Yeah, a lot of people are, Kitty. A lot are. I just can't believe where she was found and she was still in her car. She was down in that lake for over a year. Damn."

"Yeah, this is a really fucked-up situation. I just wish you all weren't the people that everyone is still side-eyeing about it."

"People are still doing that because of that picture and because we're the PGs. I wanna know who hurt *me*, though. I hate to sound insensitive but there's nothing anyone can do for Kat. I wanna know who did this to me so I won't be hurt again."

"We're gonna find out everything, Poppy, I know we are. It may take months or even years, but we will find out."

CHAPTER 29

I WIPED TEARS FROM MY EYES AS I WATCHED DARIUS' LIVE STREAM of Kat's vigil at Lake Mead since this was where her car was found as well as her body . . . and I was right out here in the parking lot in my own car. It was dark and raining, but it didn't matter because there were a lot of people here under umbrellas while their candles tried to stay lit as Mother Nature kept trying to blow them out. I didn't have the guts to go down there at all knowing that the PGs were still suspects to people in this case, but it was all confusing now since she was found in her car and not anywhere else like in a house or out in the desert, so I really didn't see myself how the PGs could be tied to this, but they obviously still were for some reason, and if Olive wasn't a hundred percent ruling them out, then I knew that I couldn't as well.

I jumped at the knocks on my window.

It was Darius.

I rolled down my window. "Hey, Darius."

"Hey, Kitty. How come you didn't come down to the vigil? I know it's raining and all, but I would've loved to see you there."

"Darius, you know I couldn't, especially now since I'm with the PGs. I know everyone is looking at me differently now especially since

I am with them even though I had nothing to do with all of this. I mean, you know how people are talking now more than ever."

"I know, Kitty. But it shows how strong all of you are to stand up to all of this. I know the PGs had nothing to do with it. They had as much to do with it as you did and you weren't even at our school last year. Seems to me that this was an unfortunate accident. It happens to people all the time."

"Yeah, that's what I hope as well." I looked and saw people staring into my rained-soaked windshield as they left the vigil to go to their cars. "Um, Darius. I'll see you at school tomorrow."

"Okay, get home safe."

"Girls, we're in a crisis here. There are people out there who still think we had something or everything to do with what'd happened to Kat, so we have to stay vigilant now more than ever, so that means we always have to be with one another. No one goes anywhere without one of us, okay?" Prima said, as we sat over at Lauren's house the next day after school.

"Well, it doesn't seem like people are thinking it was us that much anymore, Prima. Because of where Kat was found, people are now starting to believe it was an accident," Rika said.

"Yeah, but that's mainly on social media, Rika, and you know it. Social media people are obsessed with us and many other things. Even I don't have an addiction to it like I once did, and especially now," Prima said.

"Me neither," Ursula said.

"Yeah, I feel good that I'm not on there as much as I used to be," Ariana said.

"Me as well," Lauren said.

"I try to stay off but it's hard," Rika said with a grin.

"I was never a full-blown social media addict," Olive said.

"I wasn't either," I said.

"Well, regardless, we're still getting shit from people about us having something to do with it, and you see how it doesn't matter that she was found in her car submerged in the lake. We weren't at the lake that day, but we have no proof that we weren't. It's all gonna be a matter of time before we're questioned again, so we need to stay on the same page about everything, just like last year," Prima said.

"Well, I definitely don't wanna go down for something I had nothing to do with especially since I wasn't with you all when it happened," Olive firmly said.

The PGs gave her a serious look.

"Um, Olive, *we know* you weren't with us last year when this happened, okay? But the cops are gonna think we told you something about it so be prepared to be questioned as well. Kitty wasn't with us either, but I know she's gonna be questioned, so Kitty, be prepared as well," Prima warned me.

"Okay," I replied, but was not surprised.

"And, Olive, did you realize what you said?" Ursula asked her.

"What?" Olive asked.

"*You said* you weren't gonna go down for this because you weren't with us when it happened. Well, we weren't with Kat when she went into that lake with her car, but it's like you're trying to say that we were without saying it," Ursula said.

The PGs stared at Olive.

I was really curious to see what she was going to say as well because between the two of us, she did tell me she didn't a hundred percent rule the PGs out.

"Um, I never said that, Ursula, so don't go putting words into my mouth," Olive angrily said.

"Okay, stop this right now. It's clear that everyone is starting to get heated and I'm not gonna have this in my house. We all know what we need to say again when we're questioned again by the cops because we will be and it's all a matter of time that we're gonna be, so like Prima said, we need to be prepared," Lauren said.

"Has anyone talked to Poppy yet?" I asked. And I had to know this. Olive looked at me.

"No, none of us have, Kitty," Prima said. "I don't know what the hell her problem is. But if she thinks what happened to her is gonna get her off the hook with another round of questioning from the cops about Kat's case then she's seriously dreaming. Unlike you and Olive, she was in the group when this happened."

"And we all don't have anything to worry about because we all didn't do anything, so we can just relax when we're being questioned again," Ariana said.

"But remember to bring your lawyers with you," Prima advised.

My mouth dropped in shock.

"Lawyers? Why does she want us to bring our lawyers? I didn't do anything!" I said in a panic as I talked on the phone to Olive later on while I paced in my bedroom.

"Relax, Kitty. You don't have to bring a lawyer. You didn't do anything wrong and neither did I. I don't have one anyway."

"And neither do I. But if *they* didn't have anything to do with this then why do they need one even though they claim they didn't do anything?"

"Don't know, Kitty. It doesn't mean that they're guilty, but yeah, I don't think it means they're totally innocent, either. A lawyer can tell them which questions they can answer and not answer and all of that. I don't know anything about the legal system because I don't wanna be a lawyer, but that's what I'm thinking. But if we're questioned, we do have to have our parents there with us."

"I don't mind that because I feel they're wasting their time questioning me and you as well."

"Yeah, I feel it's a waste of time as well, with us at least." I changed the subject. "Um, I might as well tell you that I did go to the vigil last night down at the lake, but I didn't get out of the car because I didn't want anyone to know I was there."

"I know, I saw Darius' live-stream of it."

"And he saw me at the end of it."

"Kitty!"

"I know, I'm sorry I just didn't leave when it was over. I sat in my car in the parking lot watching his live-stream of it. I just felt I had to be there and all. I feel so bad for Kat's family and friends. They were really holding out hope that she was still alive somewhere even after a whole year had gone by. I shouldn't be treated like an enemy just because I'm with the PGs and neither should you, Olive."

"Yeah, I know we shouldn't, Kitty, but that's not the way it is. We should be the poster girls for guilt by association."

I laughed. "Yeah, we should be!" I looked at my phone since I had a call waiting.

It was Zoe!

"Olive, I gotta go. My mom just got home," I lied.

"Okay, Kitty."

"Hi, Zoe. I'm so sorry about Kat. I really am."

"Thank you, Kitty, and I really mean that. Thanks for everything you did. It's too bad she wasn't found alive."

"I know, Zoe. And I feel so bad for you and your family because you all hoped and prayed and it ended like this. I'm so sorry again."

"Well, Kat's life may have ended, but who is responsible for ending it will be caught and will begin the rest of their lives in prison. And *I know* those fuckin' bitches had everything to do with it."

"What fuckin' bitches?"

"Kitty! You know damn well I'm talking about the PGs. You may have not been here last year, but they're hiding so much shit from you about Kat that you don't even know the half of it."

"They honestly haven't told me anything, Zoe. They keep sticking to the same thing about not having anything to do with it."

"They're lying to you, Kitty. All of them are. And I know they brainwashed Olive into lying for them as well since she wasn't with them last year when this happened."

I didn't wanna tell her that Olive even said herself that she wasn't a hundred percent ruling them out, so there might be some truth to what Zoe was saying.

"Well, the PGs all know that it's all a matter of time before they're all questioned again, and I know they're gonna say the same shit they said the first time they were questioned about it over a year ago—that they had nothing to do with it. I don't believe that one single bit. Kat did not end up in that lake in her car by accident. I think they made it look like an accident."

I gasped! "You think so, Zoe?"

"I know so, Kitty. You're with a dangerous group of girls, ones who always think they're gonna get a pass in life for every bad thing they do because of their popularity. People need to stop worshipping these popular girls and that goes for all schools and even beyond school because this is pathetic. And just to think my sister wanted to be one of them so bad. I really believe that's what caused her to be killed."

"I honestly can't believe I'm hearing this, Zoe. I hope this isn't true about the PGs, but I can't rule anything out. They wanted me to be in their group because they said they wanted me to have the All-American high school experience and that there was no better group of girls to hang around. Of course I wasn't gonna turn it down. But I never, ever thought I was gonna be caught up in all of this. Never."

"I know you didn't, Kitty. But now that you unfortunately are, you need to be my spy on them. You need to tell me everything they say about Kat's case because trust me, they're gonna start talking about it again. One of them is gonna slip and say something, and you need to tell me what is said. They're not gonna be able to keep it a secret forever that they had something to do with this. I almost have a feeling now that the one who would've told the truth is the one who's no longer here, Olivia."

I found this very interesting. "Really? Why Olivia?"

"She just seemed like the type that just would—can't really explain it. I know there is definitely something behind her suicide, Kitty, and don't believe any shit the PGs tell you about it not being about Kat—I really think it was, and if you can confirm to me that it was, then at least Olivia had a conscience."

"Yeah, there have been a lot of rumors that her suicide had something to do with Kat's disappearance." I sighed. "I will try to tell you what I can, Zoe, but you know I can't ask them too many questions because they might think that I'm suspicious about something and start checking me for wires and everything, or even checking my phone."

"Oh, and speaking about phones."

"What about them?"

"Kat's phone is missing," she informed me. "She definitely had it on her that night because she called me two hours before she went missing. That was the last call I'd received from her. I know she had her phone in her car or in her purse, but it wasn't in there, they said. They searched everywhere. So whoever had something to do with what'd happened to her has her phone. The cops said that's an important piece of information that they're not letting the media know about, but I'm letting you know about it, so please, don't say anything to anyone about it."

This sent chills all over me. "I won't. I feel so overwhelmed, Zoe, I can't lie. I'll help you in any way I can, but I don't wanna get in trouble."

"You'll never get in trouble for getting who's responsible for what'd happened to Kat. Please, Kitty, we need you. You're on the inside with the PGs. Do this for me and Kat's friends and family, but especially, do it for Kat. As you know and everyone else knows, she can't tell us anything."

"I'll help you all in any way I can," I said once again.

CHAPTER 30

THE DAY OF QUESTIONING. IN MORE WAYS THAN ONE.

With what it looked like hundreds of people on both sides of the steps of the police station—some pro-PGs and some anti-PGs—they yelled all sorts of things at us as we walked in a single file line while we walked in between our parents as well as lawyers. Prima led the way with Ursula behind her; Lauren was behind Ursula, and Rika was behind Lauren. Ariana was behind Rika, and Olive was behind Ariana. I was behind Olive.

"THE NOTORIOUS PGs!"

"KILLERS!"

"LIARS!"

"WE LOVE THE PGs!"

"THE PGs ARE INNOCENT!"

And various other nice or not-so-nice things being yelled out by people who had no idea what the real story was . . . and I didn't know what it was, either.

We were only being questioned, but I felt like we were already on trial.

And we decided to follow our lawyers' advice and look like we were already on trial by dressing like we were going to court instead of to a police station just for questioning. We all wore white long-sleeved shirts in various styles, such as a simple collar or a bow-tie style, tucked into a black A-line midi skirt and black heels. We all carried the exact same Coach Tabby Top Handle bag in black, and luckily, my mom very coincidentally had this exact bag that she'd carried to work but hadn't carried it lately since she liked to rotate bags a lot. With the exception of Ariana whose hair was very short, the rest of us wore our hair in high, big, and neat buns on the top our heads, and makeup and lipstick that complemented our skin tones. We were all also instructed by our parents and lawyers—for those of us who had a lawyer—to look straight ahead and not to answer anyone or react to the nasty name-calling or even to the support we were getting.

Yeah, we looked like a bunch of freakin' clones and cameras from everywhere lit us up.

I couldn't believe I was caught up in all of this as I walked through all the melee between my parents like all of the PGs with their parents and lawyers, and I felt like I was watching myself on TV.

We were finally inside.

"My goodness! I've never experienced anything like that before in my life! I didn't realize just how guilty people think we are about this!" I said, as we all talked in one group and our parents and lawyers talked in another.

"Well, count yourself lucky, Kitty. Your assumed guilt is by association. It's messed up that it has to be this way for you, but unfortunately it's true," Prima said, as she checked herself out in her mirror.

"Well, we all can't say that we don't look beautiful because this look we all picked out is on point," Ariana said.

The PGs nodded in agreement.

"Well, we're only here for questioning, and it will be the last time we will be here because my lawyer says they have nothing to indict us on," Ursula said.

"Absolutely nothing," Rika said.

"That's why we had to look good because it will be the last time we will be here," Prima assured us.

"Yeah, I hope so," Olive said.

We all looked at her.

"What do you mean, Olive?" Lauren asked.

"Yeah, what's with the negativity, Olive? I mean, like Kitty, you're only here through guilt by association. And I know yours and Kitty's questioning is gonna be different from ours because of it," Prima said.

"It is?" I said.

"Yeah, it is," Prima reassured me. "That's what my lawyer said."

Detective Jennifer Markson walked into the hallway. "Kitty Laine?"

"Right here," I said.

"We're ready for you. Will one or both of your parents be sitting in this questioning with you?" she asked.

I looked at my parents.

"That's what we're here for," Dad said.

I looked back at all of the PGs while I walked with my parents to the interrogation room, and the look they gave me chilled me to the bone.

A minute later, we all reached the interrogation room, and this was the last time I'd hoped to see it.

"That's quite a mob out there," Dad said, as they sat down in a corner in the room while I sat at the table. "I didn't realize just how popular your group of friends really are, Kitty, but it's unfortunate that you're all in this situation."

"I don't even know why I'm here. I didn't do anything," I said, as I tried to calm my nerves.

"We know you didn't, honey. You know you're here because you're friends with the PGs. Guilt by association at its finest. The cops just wanna know if your friends told you anything about the case, that's all. We shouldn't be here all day and night," Mom said.

Detective Markson and a uniformed cop walked back in with two cups of coffee for my parents and a bottle of water for me.

"Thank you," we all said.

Markson sat down right across from me. "So, Kitty. This is the second time I'm talking to you, but the first time I'm talking to you about the Kat Black case, even though we touched on it when you were last here."

"Yes," I replied, and nervously took a sip of my water.

She looked at a picture and gently shoved it over to me. "Have the

PGs ever shown you this picture?"

It was the infamous picture of all of them with Kat Black. Now being the last confirmed picture of her alive.

"No, they haven't directly shown it to me," I honestly replied. "I've, of course, heard about it, though, and seen it on social media. But no, they've never shown it directly to me," I restated.

"Okay," she said. She pulled out a black pen and a red marker, and gently shoved it over to me. "Now, one of those girls in the picture is deceased besides the victim now, obviously. I want you to identify every girl in the picture by writing their names where they're standing at, and circle the one who's deceased and write her name as well. Also, circle the deceased victim with the red marker and identify her as well, and sign on the first line by the X."

I looked at my parents. They nodded to me as a non-verbal way of telling me to do what she said do. I identified Prima, first; Ariana, second; Poppy, third; Lauren, fourth; Rika, fifth; Ursula, sixth; and circled Olivia and wrote her name. I identified Kat, and circled her with the red marker since she was now officially a deceased victim. I signed in the black marker by the X and gently shoved the picture back over to her.

She looked at it and nodded. "Very good. Mr. and Mrs. Laine, I need your signatures on the second and third lines were the X's are since she's underage."

"No problem," Dad said, and was given the picture to sign.

My mom was handed it next and signed it as well.

"Thank you," Markson said, and put the picture back in a folder. "So, Kitty, how close are you to Zoe Black, Kat's sister?"

"Not that close. She just wanted to know if I knew anything about her sister's disappearance up until she was unfortunately found dead, and I knew she only wanted to be close to me since I'm with the PGs. I also knew she wanted me to tell her that the PGs had everything to do with it, but they told me they had nothing to do with it so I couldn't lie to her and tell her what she obviously wanted to hear. The PGs just haven't talked about this a lot. Since I didn't know any of them when this happened because I didn't even live here in this state when it did, then I can only go on what they've told me."

"I see," Markson replied. "How close are you to Olive?"

"We're very close," I said. "I connected to her almost instantly. But as you know, Olive also wasn't in the group when this happened."

"I know," she informed me. "But has she told you things about the Kat Black case that the PGs didn't want you to know?"

"Like what?"

"Like anything."

"No, she hasn't."

I told my first lie to her and in front of my parents. I felt awful.

I just couldn't tell her that Olive did mention to me about there being an alleged fight between one of the PGs and Kat the night Kat disappeared, but I just didn't understand how that alleged fight led to Kat and her car being submerged in Lake Mead. Things still weren't connecting with me when it came to all of this. I was just as confused as anyone else.

"Okay. Well, has Zoe told you anything new about the case?"

"No, she hasn't."

I just told another lie.

All thanks to Zoe, I now knew about Kat's phone not being found anywhere on her or in her car since she was found, so Zoe told me that she knew that someone obviously had it, and the person who obviously had it knew exactly what'd happened to her. I couldn't agree with that more. It was information that I knew Zoe had told Markson and she wanted to see if Zoe had told me. I also knew that this information was not given to the media since that was what Zoe told me as well. I knew she was trying to trap me into something, and I wasn't falling for it.

"Very well," Markson said.

"My goodness! I felt like I was being questioned in a full-blown trial while I was in there!" I said to Olive over the phone while comfortably in my loungewear. "I literally felt like I was on a witness stand!"

"Yeah, me too, Kitty—but that's what they do. They're cops, they have to be very thorough and any little question they ask can lead to something big. They wouldn't ask us a question that wasn't important."

"But they were making it seem as if I was more important to the case than I am."

"Kitty, I hate to tell you this, but you are more important to the case than you think you are, and so am I. They obviously know about you talking to Zoe and everything, and being close to me since I was the PG who replaced Olivia, and most of all you're a part of the PGs. It's clear that they believe that the PGs run their mouths about a lot of things, and they probably think they've done it in front of you not thinking that you'll go to the cops with everything they've said about Kat's case."

"But that's just it, all they've told me is that they didn't have anything to do with it, and who am I to say that they did? I didn't know them or you at the time. I feel like you've told me more about the case than any of them ever have."

"And I sure hope you didn't tell Markson that, Kitty."

"No, Olive, I didn't," I honestly replied. "She was trying to get it out of me, I knew she was, but she didn't get anything out of me. She didn't get anything out of me when it came to the things Zoe told me as well. I just couldn't get myself to tell her. I hated lying to her and to my parents, but I just couldn't tell what I've been told by you and Zoe. I mean, how do we know that the fight between one of the PGs and Kat really happened?"

"That's true. Could've been something made up because I just don't see how the fight and where Kat was ultimately found is connected."

"And that's exactly what I was thinking about and why I didn't even mention it. I just didn't wanna give out all of this information about it because I just don't know if it's true or not. I'm starting to believe that it isn't true."

"Yeah, Kitty, so am I."

"So, was Poppy questioned?"

"Yeah, I did ask them was she questioned and they said that two detectives were sent to her house to question her at the same time we were all being questioned, so yeah, she didn't get off the hook just because she's still unable to go places."

"Okay, that's what I was wondering."

Several minutes later after getting off the phone with Olive, I decided to check out the PG site, and sure enough, they weren't short of words:

THE POPULAR GIRLS
WHITE BLOUSES, BLACK SKIRTS, BAGS AND SHOES, AND HIGH-BUN HAIRDOS, MAKE THE PGs LOOK AS INNOCENT AS CAN BE ON THIS DAY OF QUES-TIONING!

Walking in a single file line with each one of them between their parents with their lawyers on the side —for those of them who had them, and all of them did except PG Olive and PG Kitty—the PGs walked into the police station looking like a group of goody-good girls from a boarding school with their clearly-planned, working-girl looks on completed with $550 Coach Tabby Top Handle bags.

The looks were on point and made them look very beautiful like they always are . . . .

But are they as innocent as they looked?

But this is a serious matter, and since it's been confirmed that Kat Black is in fact dead and where she was found, it's confusing as to who could've had something to do with this. But since the PGs have been some of the biggest suspects since day 1 of her disappearance, they were brought back in for ques-tioning after she was found dead in her car under water in Lake Mead on all nights, the Sahara Palms and Roses Festival after-party.

The PGs have always maintained their innocence, and none of us can really say anything because they very well may be, but some of our insiders at the police station told us that they were all asked the same questions except for PG Kitty since she didn't know of the PGs existence since she wasn't here when this happened. But nevertheless, she was questioned because there could've been some things the PGs told her that could make a case against them, but from what we know, Kitty didn't snitch if there's something that she does know about the case that the PGs told her that the cops and no one else knows.

PG Olive, who was also not a PG when this happened, was asked pretty much the same questions as all of the other PGs because she's been with them for over a year now, and her and Kitty are very close. We were told when we asked about Poppy's questioning that she was being questioned at her home the same time the other PGs were questioned at the station and was going to be asked the same questions, so she wasn't off the hook by any means because this is a whole separate case than the one she's recovering from, and we hope to see what is up with her case real soon.

But again, are the PGs really innocent as their looks portray them to be? You can all answer that in a poll below:

Are the PGs Innocent of Kat Black's Death?

YES – 73%

NO – 27%

Well, there you have it, everyone! The PGs are truly loved by their fans, but only the PGs know if the 73% is right . . . or if the 27% is right.

These poll results weren't surprising to me, either, and it showed how people really felt about us. I did believe that some people thought a person or people could do no wrong, but I still felt that even though the majority of people thought the PGs were innocent, I felt that we still weren't getting anywhere when it came to what really happened that night.

CHAPTER 31

The Night of Kat Black's Disappearance

"Hey, Zoe. It's Kat. I just wanted to let you know that I'm leaving the party early so I'm gonna be home in about two hours so let Mom and Dad know."

"Okay, Kat. I know you're excited about having your driver's license and all, but you know how pissed they get if you're not home by your curfew."

"Well, they need to lighten up because I'm responsible. I'm just gonna hang out with Willa for a while; don't know where we're going."

"Okay. Just be home in two hours because you know how they get if you're not."

"Yeah, yeah, I know. Bye."

"Bye, Kat."

While she drove down the street alone, she spotted the PGs hanging out at a mini mall. She drove into the parking lot towards them.

"Who's that?" Ariana asked.

"It looks like Kat," Lauren said.

166

"Oh, God! Is she ever gonna leave us alone? Let's go!" Ursula said.

"No, actually, let's stay and see what she wants," Prima suggested. "And, Olivia, I think you're the one of all people who should really want to talk to her."

"Yeah, I guess it's now or never," Olivia said.

Kat got out of her car and walked over to the PGs. "Hey, PGs, what's up?"

"Hanging out. What does it look like?" Prima asked.

The PGs laughed; Kat tried to smile but was embarrassed.

"Why did you steal my man from me?" Olivia said, already on the defense.

"Whoaaaaa! Uh, oh! You have some explaining to do, Kat!" Prima said.

"Yeah, you sure do!" Poppy said with a laugh.

"That's right, Olivia! No small talk, just cut right to it!" Rika said.

"Brennen said he was through with you, Olivia, so I didn't steal him from you," Kat said.

"Um, no, bitch. No. He never broke up with me; and then I see the two of you all over each other on social media with you talking all of that shit about if you're never gonna be a PG then at least you were able to get one of their men and it was *my* man! *That's* what you said, but now there's no social media standing between us so now you say it to my face!" Olivia said.

"YEAH!" the PGs said.

"Look, I'm sorry about saying that, okay?" Kat said.

"No, you're not sorry at all," Olivia said.

"Okay, fine, I'm not," Kat said angrily.

"Excuse me?" Olivia said.

"I'm not sorry then, Olivia. I'm not gonna stand here and keep saying I'm sorry to you. Who they hell are you? Who the hell are all of you? You all think you're better than all the rest of the girls like me out here because you're a PG?"

"Yeah, and it's something you wanna be so bad that you begged and begged us to be one, bitch!" Olivia said.

"That's right!" the PGs said.

"No thanks. I don't want to be a PG anymore. You guys are not worth being around. You're not as great as you think you all are, and Olivia couldn't even keep her man because he was sick of her uppity PG shit," Kat said.

"You better shut the fuck up right now, bitch! I mean it!" Olivia warned.

"Make me, bitch!" Kat said.

"Yeah, make her, Olivia! Go on!" Prima encouraged her.

"Yeah, don't let her talk that shit in front of you and in front of all of us!" Ursula said.

"What are you afraid of, Olivia? Go on and get her ass!" Poppy said.

"I'm not afraid of anything!" Olivia said, as she stood in the same place with her arms crossed in front of her.

"Looks like you're scared to me," Kat said. "And there's only one of me standing here."

"I'm not scared of you, bitch!" Olivia said.

The PGs watched intensely at what Olivia's next move was gonna be.

Olivia shook her head as she still stood in the same spot with her arms crossed. "Nah, I don't need to fight this loser bitch. She's just a sad, miserable, jealous cunt who's mad because she'll never be a PG like me; like the rest of us. You all can see that she's a drunk and high whore as well. The only power in this world she ever felt like she had was stealing my boyfriend, and that was fine because it's clear he prefers loose sluts that are only good for one thing."

Kat punched Olivia in her face!

The PGs all screamed as the fight was on!

"Get her, Olivia! Get the bitch!" the PGs yelled.

Olivia and Kat continued to fight and Olivia knocked Kat's phone out of her hand and it crashed to the ground and they eventually did as well as they continued to fight each other hard.

"This is enough!" Lauren said, as she ran over to try and break them up, but was stopped by Prima.

"No, this is Olivia's fight. Let her do what she has to do. This has been a long time coming. GET HER, OLIVIA!" Prima yelled.

Olivia and Kat had each other by the hair.

"LET GO OF MY HAIR, BITCH!" Kat yelled.

"YOU LET GO OF MINE, BITCH!" Olivia yelled back.

They let go of each other's hair and got back up on their feet, and Olivia punched Kat so hard in the face that she stumbled towards her car and hit her head on the driver's side rearview mirror and collapsed back down to the ground!

"Holy shit!" the PGs said in shock.

"Okay, the fight is really over now!" Lauren said, and went over to Olivia to try and calm her down, as Ariana and Rika helped her.

Kat looked startled as she held the back of her head as she stumbled to her feet. "Fuckin' bitch! You're gonna get it for this!" she warned as she breathed heavy, and then got in her car and drove off.

The PGs looked at each other.

"Let's get the hell out of here, too. I have to be home soon anyway," Prima said.

The PGs woke up the next day to a flood of messages:

Anyone seen Kat?

Kat didn't come home last night, her sister Zoe and parents are saying.

Kat was last seen with the PGs last night and hasn't been seen since.

And hundreds more just like them.

Then, the media texts came in:

Sahara Palms High School sophomore Kat Black missing. Please call police for any information on her whereabouts.

And hundreds more just like it.

The PGs met with each other over Prima's house.

"Look, we can't say that we saw Kat last. When she left, she could've very well went to see someone else. I know it's gonna look like we have everything to do with why she didn't go home last night, but we didn't. We didn't follow her after the fight she had with you, Olivia, so we have no idea where she went because we were all in my mom's SUV," Prima said.

"I know, but what if we *were* the last people she was with?" Olivia said. "I feel so bad, you guys. She made me so mad and embarrassed me even more in front of all of you that I couldn't stand there and take that shit from her. But when she hit me, all bets were off. I was already still angry about her stealing Brennen from me, but she stood there and rubbed and rubbed that shit in my face while you all were standing there. She did that shit to humiliate me and made me look like a weak-ass bitch in front of you all, and that took a lot of guts because the bitch was there all by herself. It was seven against one."

"And it was your fight with her, Olivia, not any of ours. We weren't gonna help you fight her and it was clear that you didn't need any of us to," Ursula said.

"And that last punch really knocked the wind out of her! She knew she couldn't fight after that!" Prima said.

"Yeah, that's why she got in her car and screeched off," Poppy said.

"Well, I hope they find her soon. But she did seem drunk last night, and people are saying all over social media that she was at a house party she'd obviously came from before she saw us. When she was talking, she smelled like alcohol," Lauren said.

"Yeah, that's what I noticed, too," Rika said.

"So I wasn't just smelling things because it smelled that way to me, too," Ariana said.

"Yeah, come to think of it, it did," Prima said.

"And that's how she got the courage to talk that shit and picked that fight with you, Olivia. She was drunk and probably high as well. No one in their right state of mind would act like that when they know that many people are against them," Ursula said.

"I know they wouldn't," Olivia said. "But I didn't think she would be missing right now."

"She'll turn up, and when she does, there can be a round two!" Prima said with a laugh.

The PGs laughed as they nodded in agreement.

Two months after Kat's Disappearance

"Look, girls. It's clear that she's missing because I just think she would've been found by now. Where the hell is she?!" Olivia said in a panic.

"We don't know, Olivia. Look, like we said two months ago, we have no idea where she drove off to after you had that fight with her. The cops didn't need to know that you got into that fight with her and I'm glad all of us agreed not to mention it. Someone obviously took a picture of us standing there at the mini mall that night talking to her; it means nothing because it proves nothing. Where she went after that fight with you, only she knows," Prima said.

"I think she's still alive. She's just doing this for attention. She's just trying to get us in trouble," Poppy said.

"I agree," Ursula said.

"And you know I definitely agree," Prima said.

"Well, she was obviously drunk, so who knows where she went," Ariana said. "But we had nothing to do with it."

"I have to agree with Olivia. I think she would've been found by now. Two months is a long time to be gone and not be in contact with anyone. She would've tried to contact someone by now," Lauren said.

"Well, we didn't have anything to do with it, and the cops knew that so that's why they let us all go. If we really knew where she was at then they would sense it in us, you know? And would've given us lie detector tests and all that," Rika said.

The PGs nodded in agreement.

"This is just so fucked up, it just is!" Olivia said. "I feel so bad now. I still don't like her at all, but this is just crazy. I hit her so hard where she hit her head on the side rearview mirror of her car. I wish I never did that."

"She hit you first, Olivia, remember that. You were defending your-self," Prima reminded her.

"That's right," the PGs said.

"Yeah, I was defending myself," Olivia said, as tears welled up in her eyes. "But how do we know if Kat was able to defend herself after she drove off from us? Anything could've happened to her."

The PGs all looked at each other.

"And we had nothing to do with it. Always remember that," Prima said.

"I just feel responsible, I just do," Olivia said as tears streamed from her eyes. "I don't think I'm ever gonna get over this. I just don't have a good feeling about this. I don't think she's ever gonna be found."

Three days later, Olivia committed suicide by overdosing on prescription medication.

CHAPTER 32

The PGs and I stood outside of Prima's home. With uniformed and plain-clothed cops standing beside us and a sea of media in front of us, we were here to make an official statement to put all rumors to rest in the case of Kat Black.

"Hi, everyone. I'm Prima Donna Queensridge. I know that all of you are here today to get a response from me, as well as all of my friends here, about the Kat Black case. We are pleased to confirm with everyone that there will be no charges filed against any of us in this case, and that Kat's unfortunate untimely demise has been ruled as accidental. We hope that everyone will respect the decision that the authorities have made in this matter because it is the correct one. Thank you."

"I'm Ursula Steele. I'm very happy that there has been a conclusion to this case and people are no longer misinformed about what happened that night. We told the truth both times when we had to talk to the authorities about it and fortunately they believed us because we were in fact telling the truth. My friends and I just want everyone to be informed about the truth, and now everyone is. Thank you."

"I'm Ariana Garcia. I'm happy to know that we were believed in this case. It has been hard enough on us, but I know nothing has been as hard as what Kat's family and friends had to go through for a little over a year not knowing her whereabouts. I wish it would've been a better outcome, but I know she's in a better place. I just don't want people believing things that weren't true about this case, and I'm glad the authorities were able to put all rumors, speculations, and theories to rest. Thank you."

Lauren sighed as she got ready to speak next. "I'm Lauren Dawson. My heart still hurts for Kat's family and friends, and it always will. I believe in telling the truth no matter how much it may hurt someone to do so and no matter how much it may affect someone. We knew the truth and we told the truth. What happened to Kat I wouldn't wish on my worst enemy. No one should have to go through what she went through, and no family or friends should have to endure the pain of losing a loved one for the rest of their lives from an unfortunate acci-dent. May God give them the strength to carry on with their lives. Thank you."

"I'm Rika Nitzu. I'm very happy this case has been solved. It wasn't the outcome that people had hoped with Kat being found alive, but I'm glad her family finally knows what happened to her and how it happened, and I'm glad that no false charges are being filed against us. We have been through enough already because of people thinking we had something to do with all of this when this was an unfortunate accident, so I hope that people will respect how the authorities came to their conclusions and stop all of this harassing of us. Thank you."

Olive was the next to speak. "I'm Olive Lowes. I'm in a unique position when it comes to this case because I was not with the PGs at the time this occurred. But when I became a part of their group, they told me exactly what'd happened because they wanted me to hear it straight from them instead of from the unreliable and disreputable social media, because everyone knows how it is on there. I believed every word they told me and knew they didn't have anything to do with it. I would not have wanted to be a part of their group if I had a one percent doubt that they weren't telling me the truth. I have prayed for Kat's family since the day she disappeared and still pray for them and always will because no one should have to go through this. Thank you."

I was next. And once again, I looked like a deer caught in a pair of semi-truck headlights, even though I knew I had to speak about this today like all of the other PGs. "Um, hi. I'm Kitty Laine. I'm very happy that the authorities were finally able to solve this case, and that no charges are being filed against my friends or me. Like Olive, I wasn't with the group when this happened. I've only been with them a short time now I still feel, so all of this still feels so surreal to me. I knew the PGs didn't lie to me when they told me personally that they had nothing to do with Kat's unfortunate disappearance, and they were proven by the authorities to be right. I also pray for Kat's family, and I hope that no one ever has to go through anything like this again, the PGs or any family, because I believe that it took a toll on everyone in one way or the other. Thank you."

"Thank you, ladies," Detective Jennifer Markson said. "And just to let you all—the media—know, I haven't received an official statement from Poppy Hendrichs, the family of the late Olivia Mahoney, or from Kat Black's family about this case. I will update you all on our social media pages if statements from any of them come in, or you can try and get statements from them yourselves. Thank you all for coming."

"Wow, just as soon as this case started, it seems like it's over so fast," Ursula said, as we all sat in the backyard of Prima's house by the pool. It was already in the freakin' 90's out here and it was only spring. Unheard of where I was from.

"Well, a year does go by very fast," Rika said. "And I meant every word of what I said about how this harassment against us better stop, because we're no killers and no liars like how all of those idiots who are a part of that Kat Kult said about us."

"Well, no one is saying anything now," Ariana said, and sipped on her non-alcoholic tropical drink. "We had no charges against us because we told the truth—we didn't do anything. It wasn't our fault she obviously took a wrong turn and ended up in Lake Mead. She was drunk and high and upset because of the fight she got in with Olivia, and we knew that and that's what unfortunately happens to people who put themselves in those situations."

"Exactly right, Ariana. She shouldn't have been driving. She knew better," Prima said, and sipped on her drink.

"She definitely wasn't in the right state of mind. I saw that when she seemed to have showed so much courage against Olivia when she had six friends to back her up and she didn't have any. I just wish Olivia didn't feel so bad about fighting her and thinking it led to what'd happened to her," Lauren said.

"Yeah, exactly, because those were choices she made to be drunk and high and thought she could fight and then thought she could just drive home after," Prima said.

"But she did hit her head hard on her side rearview mirror after Olivia punched her in the face," Lauren said.

"Well, Olivia didn't know Kat was gonna hit her head on it. Kat picked the fight, so she should've known that you don't know what's gonna happen to you when you are in one. She stopped fighting because she knew she was starting to lose so she got in her car and drove off," Ursula said.

"Yeah, and unfortunately into the lake," Lauren said.

Olive sighed. "I'm just still wondering why Poppy didn't make a statement."

We all looked at her.

"Well, I'm at a point now where I don't give a fuck what Poppy does or doesn't do. Because she acts as if she still can't talk to us, she's skating on very thin ice with us. If she doesn't start talking to us soon then she's gonna be looking for some new friends," Prima warned.

I gasped, as did all of the other PGs. "Are you serious, Prima?" I had to ask.

"Yeah, I am, Kitty. I've had enough of her shit and so have the rest of you, right?" Prima said.

"Right," the PGs replied.

"Well, maybe she just needs more time to recover. She went through a harrowing ordeal. The Kat Black case may be closed, but Poppy's is still wide open," Olive said.

"Yeah, and she's acting like we're her enemies now since this happened to her. All of this shit we've done for her and everything and she wants to be like this? She better talk to us and I mean talk to us soon because if she doesn't, she's gonna find herself being a very lonely person very soon," Prima warned.

We all looked at each other. She was serious. I knew I had to talk to Poppy soon.

CHAPTER 33

Later at home, I couldn't miss what the PG blog said about what'd happened today:

THE POPULAR GIRLS
BREAKING NEWS
NO CHARGES FILED AGAINST THE PGs IN THE KAT
BLACK CASE
DEATH RULED AN "UNFORTUNATE ACCIDENT"

Well, we can't say that this is surprising. To the 73% of you who thought the PGs were innocent in this case, well, it's clear that the authorities agreed with you. And we can say here that we have to agree with the conclusion as well. There was absolutely nothing connecting the PGs to how Kat's car ended up in Lake Mead, and her body was so badly decomposed that they couldn't get anything from it, so they just concluded that she may have gotten distracted and made a wrong turn into the lake. There are still speculations that she was drunk and high and that she did have a problem with drugs and alcohol, and that might have been the case, but it's clear that the PGs had nothing to do with it as they originally stated, so it looks like all of the people who have been messing with them and accusing them of doing this owes them a formal apology.

We really loved how each PG spoke about their thoughts about no charges being filed against them, and they were all well-spoken and seemed to have had no hard feelings about having been questioned twice about it as well as having red paint thrown all over them and their cars spray-painted with "Killer" and "Liar" on it.

There wasn't a statement issued from PG Poppy, or the late PG Olivia's family, nor from Kat's family, and we have a feeling that there won't be. But the PGs have been through enough when it comes to this, and we feel that they handled it all with class. There's a reason why so many people love them.

But it's clear that not everyone loves them, because PG Poppy is still recovering from what'd happened to her in the school bathroom some time ago, and now we're thinking this has absolutely nothing to do with the Kat Black case. Something is going on in the relationship of the PGs and PG Poppy as well from what we're hearing, so we're looking forward to finding out more information about this when more becomes available, because there is never a shortage of drama when it comes to the PGs!

I knew this site was already sensing something about the relationship between Poppy and the PGs, and they would love to know what Prima said today about her, but I wasn't gonna tell them anything since Prima told me I was not allowed to talk to them unless they all talked to them, so I knew I needed to keep my mouth shut.

My phone rang.

It was Zoe!

"Hi, Zoe."

"Hey, Kitty. I just wanted to let you know that I'm not mad at you for making a statement about no charges being filed against any of you today. I don't like the conclusion to this, but my family and I said we're not gonna fight it and that we have accepted it, and we just have to move on because we know that this is what Kat would want us to do."

"I know this is what she would want you all to do, too."

"The only thing I want back is her phone because I feel that's a big connection to her, but at this point, I just don't know if anyone actually has it so I don't know if it will ever be found."

"I'm so sorry about that, Zoe. I wish I did know where it was. And it's clear that the media is keeping with their promise about not mentioning it to everyone. What if someone does have it? Will it change the outcome of the case?"

"That's what the authorities will have to decide. But for right now, it's still lost somewhere, and it may not ever be found."

"I'm sorry, Zoe."

"It's okay, Kitty. You did a lot when it came to Kat. You didn't even know her and you came to two vigils for her, and you always talked to me when I wanted to talk to you, so I thank you so much for all of it. I'm not ever going back to Sahara Palms, so I won't be seeing you there. I just wanna let you know that I appreciate everything you've done, even though like I said, the outcome wasn't what my family and Kat's friends had hoped for, but it is what it is. We're not ready to make a statement about it like they wanted us to do and we probably never will be. We just wanna move on like we all know Kat would want us to do. She wasn't a perfect person—had a problem already with alcohol and drugs and she was only sixteen—but she was a person, and she was loved and respected by her family and friends. And I'm glad that someone from the group that was accused of having something to do with her disappearance was willing to risk being kicked out of it just for talking to me. Thank you again, Kitty."

My eyes welled up with tears. "You're welcome, Zoe. Um, there's something that I need to know."

"What is it?"

"Do you have any idea who could've vandalized the PGs' cars in the school lot that day? Because it's clear whoever did it thought the PGs were killers and liars and they have been proven not to be."

She sighed. "You promise you won't tell?"

I gasped! "No! I won't tell at all! Who did it?"

"Willa and her boyfriend and his best friend. She asked me did I wanna help them and I told them no; I wanted nothing to do with it, and I really didn't think they were gonna do it until she showed me the pictures. Willa has been so distraught about Kat that she transferred to another school, but hasn't told anyone what school she goes to, but it's not an online school. Her boyfriend and best friend are out of high school; graduated last year from different schools. She said she needed to get back at the PGs for what she felt they did and had gotten away with, but I guess it was all for nothing since they didn't kill Kat after all. Please don't tell them I told you, okay?"

"I won't," I promised. "They don't need to know everything. Their cars are fixed and showroom new; they just have it like that. Wow, I'm just glad they didn't vandalize mine!"

"They said they weren't going to do that, Kitty, since you had nothing to do with what'd happened."

"Yeah, I didn't. Well, I really hope we can stay in touch even though you don't go to Sahara Palms anymore."

"We will, Kitty. I have to go now. Take care."

"You too, Zoe."

Tears streamed down from my eyes as I passively watched TV. It was sad that her family didn't get the outcome they wanted, but I didn't want the PGs ultimately charged with her disappearance and now her untimely demise. And Zoe was right, no one was perfect, but Kat didn't deserve to die the way she did. I felt so bad for her family and knew I always would.

My phone rang again.

It was Olive.

"Hey, Olive."

"Hey, Kitty! I'm *so relieved* we aren't having any charges filed against us. I can finally sleep good tonight."

"Yeah, you're telling me. It's been hard on me as well and like you, I had nothing to do with it. But yeah, even though we didn't, we're a part of the PGs which means we could've gotten in trouble if they'd told us they had something to do with what'd happened to Kat and we didn't contact the cops about it."

"Yeah, you're right, Kitty."

"So, do you know why Poppy didn't wanna give a statement?"

"No, she still acts as if she doesn't wanna answer our calls, and she's pushing Prima closer and closer to the breaking point."

"I don't wanna see Prima break or anyone else in the PGs break. It was hard enough for all of us not to break during everything that was going on, so I need a break from all of this shit. I feel so relieved like you that no charges are being filed against any of us for what'd happened to Kat and now her case is officially closed, but then I thought about Poppy. Hers is a whole new case. We still don't know who hurt her and, Olive, she hasn't told me anything about who she thinks could've done this because she truly doesn't know, and I believe her."

"Well, she was unconscious for who knows how long, so I believe her, too."

"I hope it doesn't take us long to find out who hurt Poppy because she's still really upset about it."

"Yeah, and she's taking it out on the wrong people."

"I agree, Olive. Maybe she's wondering why it happened to her and not to any of you."

"Well, stuff did happen to us when it came to Kat's case, but we don't know what all Poppy has been doing and who she's bullied. She's leaving a lot of stuff out that she needs to come clean about and she knows it."

I found this very interesting. "Well, if that's the case then I hope she does. There's a reason why she was hurt, and I hope she's able to find out who did this to her."

"And if she doesn't talk to us then we can't help her," Olive concluded.

"Well, hopefully she will talk to you all soon. I think she just still needs time to recover in all aspects."

"I know, but she wasn't the only one who's been through a lot and she knows it."

"Yeah, I know she knows it, Olive, and you're right when it comes to what she was doing to people before she got hurt. I honestly thought it was tied to Kat's case, but now I just don't believe that it is. Maybe I can just talk to her by myself since it seems like I'm the only one she's been reaching out to. I really wanna know why she's acting as if she doesn't wanna talk to any of you, and that's what I mainly wanna know. I'll try not to ask too many questions because I admit this is bugging me about why she's being this way and why she still doesn't wanna talk to any of you since this has happened. This is definitely not how you treat your friends."

"It isn't, Kitty. So, you do what you need to do and ask when you talk to her. Because if she keeps this up then she's not gonna have any friends at all because she knows damn well nothing tops being a PG."

Considering what we've all been through, it seems safer not to be one, I thought. "Yeah, nothing tops it," I said.

CHAPTER 34

"Okay, girls. We have a little more than a month and a half left of school for this year, so we need to figure out if we wanna still continue to have Poppy with us or not. She's being a total bitch about all of this as if we haven't gone through shit ourselves. Since she still refuses to talk to us or see us, then we need to make some decisions here," Prima said.

The PGs looked at each other while I stared in shock. I honestly didn't think they were really thinking about kicking her out of the group because she hadn't been talking to any of them. I wanted to tell them I was talking to her and I was a part of the group, but I didn't know if Poppy wanted me to let them know that, or I didn't know if they would turn on me in some weird way because I was talking to her but she still didn't want to talk to them.

"Um, maybe we need to give her more time. She's been through a lot," I said.

"Oh, and we haven't?" Prima said.

"Well, I have to agree with Kitty," Lauren said. "We may have had a lot of things happen to us, but none of us were badly beaten like her. Maybe it was something she did to someone that she never told anyone about. We all know that she's the group's bully, and we didn't like it at all. Some people just snap, and I think whoever beat her that bad did just that."

"Sounds possible," Ariana said. "There's been a lot of rumors going around about it."

"Yeah, but who would've done this? She bullied a lot of people," Rika said.

"That's the thing," Ursula said. "She did bully a lot of people so it could've been anyone. I honestly don't know where to begin to narrow it down."

"Well, like Lauren said, she's the group's bully and we never agreed to her being like this because that's not how we wanted ourselves to be represented. We've even talked to her about it and about the fact that we're anti-bullying, but she acted as if she didn't wanna listen to us, so I feel that if she did bully someone and they got revenge on her, then I'm sorry, she got what she should've known was eventually coming," Olive said.

"I agree," Prima said.

"Me too," Ursula said.

"Well, we all agree to that, but she doesn't know that we feel this way, so what we really need to know is if one of the people she bullied did do this to her, then why is she acting as if she wants to be mad at us about it?" Rika asked.

"That's the question," Lauren said.

"Well, I feel that maybe she is because she feels like we weren't there for her?" Ariana said.

"But why would we be there for her when she put this on herself? It doesn't matter if she's a PG. We don't like bullying at all, so if she was badly beaten by a person she bullied—and we all think that she was—then she's on her own with this shit. Should the person face charges? It all depends. Poppy has always had that attitude of being the type that always wants to do what she wants to do. I mean, we all have that attitude in us, I'll admit, but none of us are as bad as her," Prima said.

"Plus, we've warned her about the bullying and all, and she obviously continued to do it and she seemed to have always gotten away with it just because she's a PG. You know, we only found out these stories on the PG blog when a person who claimed that Poppy bullied them would tell them about it, but they would always remain anonymous so we never knew who they were," Ursula said.

"Exactly. And when we would confront her about it, she would say that she either didn't do anything or that the person who made the claims against her was overexaggerating. Well, someone wanted to get revenge on her for this. She's obviously not telling her parents the whole story of why what'd happened to her happened," Prima said.

"Most definitely sounds like it," Rika said.

"Well, I just thought of something, girls," Prima said. She picked up her phone. "We're all gonna call her right now. *Right now*."

I gasped. I didn't think this was a good idea but didn't wanna say anything.

The PGs nodded in agreement.

"Okay, I'm gonna try first. And then we're gonna wait for five to ten minutes and then another one of us are gonna try and call her. I want us all together to prove to her and to each other that she hasn't been answering any of our calls," Prima said. "Okay, everyone be quiet," she said, as she put the phone in front of her and clearly had it on speaker so we all could hear.

Poppy's phone rang several times.

No answer.

Prima hung up. "Okay, who's next?"

"I'll go," Ursula said, and called her and put her phone on speaker in front of her so everyone could hear, and all we heard was ringing.

No answer.

Rika was next, then Lauren, then Ariana, then Olive.

Same for them as it was for Prima and Ursula.

No answer.

"Kitty, now you try," Prima said.

I took a deep breath. I called her and did like all of the PGs before me—I put my phone on speaker in front of me so everyone could hear.

"Hey, Kitty," Poppy said!

We all gasped!

I looked around the room and the PGs looked shocked, all of them, and I couldn't say that I blamed them. But this showed me that this was real. The PGs weren't lying about this. Poppy really was intentionally not answering their calls and didn't wanna see them, and the big question was why?

Why?

"Hey, Poppy," I said. "How are you?"

"I'm okay. I'm not the best, but I'm still trying to hang in there," she replied.

Prima put her index finger up to her mouth as the famous non-verbal way of telling everyone to be quiet.

"Um, were you busy just a few minutes ago?" I asked.

"No, I wasn't. I'm just sitting here watching random YouTube videos," she replied.

I looked at the PGs for what else to say because I didn't wanna say anything I wasn't supposed to. But I could see that they were very mad that she answered my call and not any of theirs, but there was a reason why and now more than ever, I was determined to find out.

Prima signaled for me to end the call.

"Well, Poppy, I have to go. I'll talk to you later."

"Okay. Bye," she said.

"Bye," I said, and ended the call. I sat with my head lowered. I didn't know what to say.

Everyone seemed to have been shocked into silence for a few seconds because you could hear a pin drop on Prima's white luxury carpet.

"Yeah, okay. We got her. Now it's official that it's true that she's intentionally ignoring us," Prima said.

I could see it all in her eyes and body language that she was trying very hard to contain her composure, as well as the other PGs.

"So, what are we gonna do about her?" Rika asked.

We all looked at Prima to see what she was going to say because I really wanted to know for myself.

Prima got up and paced around her room. "Well, first of all, we need to know why she talked to Kitty instead of to the rest of us. It was clear that she saw all of our calls but didn't answer them, but she answered Kitty's."

Everyone looked at me.

"Um, I don't know," I honestly replied. "I thought I wouldn't get a response from her like the way you all didn't get one."

But I knew I was getting responses from Poppy for weeks now, and in some cases she called me first, but I wasn't sure if I wanted to tell them that because they were mad she hadn't talked to them yet.

"Well, I think we need to decide what we wanna do with her right now," Ursula said. "Because as far as I'm concerned, if she's gonna continue to play these games with us like this then she's gonna have a very lonely senior year, and that is the worst year you can be lonely in. We're not even seniors yet and everyone knows that."

The PGs nodded in agreement.

"Well, I think a decision should be made with her right here in front of us so she can see that we mean what we say," Prima said.

"But she's obviously not talking to us," Ariana said.

"Oh, she's gonna talk to us whether she likes it or not and if she doesn't, she's gonna have a very lonely senior year like Ursula said, and we're gonna see to that if that's the last thing we do. I don't know who the hell she thinks she is now. We've all been through shit and she acts like she's above the rest of us in terms of what she's been through? I don't think so. She's gonna see that this is not how she treats people she calls her friends!" Prima declared.

Prima had a certain fire in her eyes that gave me chills. I'd never seen her like this. I was now very afraid for Poppy . . . and for myself.

"Olive, I'm afraid now. I think we've been through so much in such a short amount of time and now all of this shit is starting up again because of Prima's threats about Poppy if she doesn't talk to all of you. I feel like I'm right in the middle of all of this shit once again. I just don't know what I wanna do," I said, as we talked on the phone later on.

"Well, Kitty, I think you know it would be best to stick with all of us. You'll be safer that way. There's always drama when it comes to us, hell, that's just life in general. But I have to side with the PGs when they say that Poppy put this on herself. She's always doing shit that would end up getting her in trouble, and she always thought she would get out of it because she's a PG. I think someone that she bullied hurt her, and if they did, she got what she should've known was coming to her like what I said earlier. But I can't help but to believe that there is something way more to all of this than the PGs want to admit, and especially what Poppy wants to admit."

I gasped. "What is it, Olive?"

"That's just it. I just don't know what it is. It's not coming to me yet but it's something, Kitty. You know, I honestly don't think you have anything to do with this, that's why Poppy is talking to you. I think she wants to tell you something but is too afraid to tell you right now. I was the closest to her until what'd happened to her had happened, but now after what'd happened to her she acts like she doesn't wanna talk to me, either, as if she doesn't trust me anymore? I'm finding it very hard to keep liking her at this point. I'm trying to give her a chance to talk to us and tell us what's going on, but I have to agree with Prima and the rest of the PGs, if she keeps this up then she's not gonna be with us anymore."

"That's why I think all of you should sit down and talk this out. Not at school but at one of your homes, or even at a place like Starbucks. I know the incident happened at school, but it's clear that someone at school did this to her. I don't understand for the life of me why she's turning her back on her friends when you all have done everything you can for her and even held that vigil for her."

"Because she's an ungrateful bitch."

"I can understand why you and the rest of the PGs would feel that way, and I'm not saying that you all shouldn't at this point. But why she's talking to me but acts like she doesn't wanna talk to any of you is definitely something you all need to talk to her about whether she wants to or not. There's obviously a reason why she's ignoring you all. I'm not gonna lie, I was shocked when she acted like that earlier today. I was actually nervous when Prima decided to have all of you take turns calling her. I was so nervous when she got to me and was hoping Poppy wouldn't answer because I knew I'd been keeping in touch with her, but when she answered I felt like hanging up."

"Yeah, I could see the look in your eyes as well as all the rest of them. But their look was different than yours because they were truly shocked that she answered your call and not any of theirs. I tried to look shocked but I wasn't surprised since I knew you'd been talking to her."

"I just want the whole group together again. I know Poppy's case is a new case, but we can't help her unless she lets us. I mean, I would think that she would've told me information about it by now, but now I believe she hasn't because she just knows that I'm gonna tell you all, and she's right—why wouldn't I tell you all?"

"I know, Kitty. But yeah, Prima's serious and so are all of the other PGs about her status if she doesn't talk to us soon. There's gonna be no more of this childish shit about acting as if she doesn't wanna talk to us anymore. She can't stay a PG and thinks she can continue to ignore us. None of us are having it."

"And I can't blame any of you for that," I said.

After I got off of the phone with Olive, I couldn't help but look at the PG site, and it looked as if they had gotten a hold of what was currently going on in with the PGs:

<u>THE POPULAR GIRLS</u>
WHAT IS GOING ON WITH THE PGs?

Okay, we are the world's number one PG gossip blog, and our sources are telling us that something major is happening in the PGs, meaning that there is a lot of talk about PG Poppy. Ever since her horrible incident in the one of the girl's bathrooms at her school, PG Poppy has remained out of touch with the other PGs, and what our sources told us, that's all of them except for PG Kitty. She has been talking to her but we don't know what she's discussed with her, but it seems like something serious if she seems to want to confide only in PG Kitty and not the rest of them, especially since she's new to the group and hasn't been with them for that long at all. So why would she trust the new PG and not any of the other ones?

With the Kat Black case behind them, the PGs seem to have a whole new set of problems with one of their own when right now, they should be sticking together the most because of it and finding out who hurt one of their own, but PG Poppy has totally cut them off since she hasn't seen them or spoken to any of them except for PG Kitty since her incident, and according to our sources, the PGs are very mad about it, in fact so mad, they said they are in the process of making a "major decision" regrading PG Poppy's status with them if she doesn't reach out to them soon, and of course, we know this just doesn't sound good, especially at a time like this when PG Poppy should be leaning on her friends the most.

What the hell is going on?

PG Kitty, as always, you are welcomed to contact us at any time to tell us what is going on with your friends, because we hate to hear that you all are in this situation considering the fact of what you all have been through.

"I wish I could tell you all, but I just can't, and even if I could, there is nothing to tell because Poppy hasn't even told me why she's not talking to them right now. Something is definitely going on, and it's clear that if Poppy is talking to me then it has nothing to do with me," I said to the screen as if I was directly talking to them.

CHAPTER 35

"That was a great workout in Gym today," I said to Prima with a smile as I toweled myself off while we walked back into the locker room. "I've never used a kettlebell before."

"Yeah, it's just as good as using any type of weight so I have it in my rotation when I work out at home by myself or with the other PGs. We usually have workout dates since we all have an exercise room in our homes, Kitty, and of course you're invited to them now since you're with us, but we haven't had any dates lately because of everything that's been going on, but we'll start up again soon."

"I look forward to it," I replied with a smile.

We approached our lockers.

I opened mine and looked at my phone. There was a text from Poppy:

Hey, Kitty. I know you're in 8th period right now because of the time, so I wanted to catch you before you left school today and because I wanna know if you wanna come over my house after you leave school today. I really, really need to talk to you and now I feel that this is the right time so I just can't wait anymore. Let me know as soon as you get this.

I looked at Prima as she went over to the showers to take a quick shower like she mostly did. I hurried and texted Poppy back:

Hi, Poppy, nice to hear from you. Yes, I'll be there.

I waited for a few seconds and her text came in almost right away:

Great, Kitty. And please, don't tell any of the PGs that you're seeing me today.

Okay, Poppy. I won't.

"Wow, your backyard is incredible, Poppy. It looks like a tropical paradise," I said, as we sat in expensive-looking lounge chairs as we sipped on our Starbucks drinks that I went to go pick up for us before I came here.

"Thank you, Kitty," she said with a smile, and took a sip of her drink. "I've been spending a lot of time out here lately."

I smiled as I stared at her. "You're healing up nicely, Poppy. It looks as if nothing has happened to you."

She nodded with a smile. "Thanks, Kitty. It may look that way from the outside, but on the inside, I just don't know if I'm ever gonna be healed."

I tensed up. I knew there was a reason why she invited me over here, and I was about to find out. "Why don't you think you're ever gonna be healed on the inside as well, Poppy? I know things haven't been great and all, but I feel things are getting better with the Kat Black case behind us and all."

"Well, there's still more to that case, Kitty, a lot more, in fact."

I gasped. "Do I even want to know?"

"Well, let's just say this, Kitty. We did tell them the truth, but what we didn't tell them was that Olivia and Kat had gotten into a fight that night—that's the part we left out when we were questioned both times, and that's a very huge part to leave out. Very huge. We stuck to the script a year ago when she first went missing, and weeks ago when she was found. And even though I wasn't there during the second round of questioning, the cops were here when they said they were gonna be and I stuck to the script as well."

"But why did you all leave that part out? That was huge, like you said."

"We just felt they didn't need to know it. I know they should've, but even with that information, it still didn't mean we were responsible for what'd happened to Kat."

"Yeah, you're right, but it still should've been mentioned, I feel."

She sighed. "Yeah, you're right, Kitty, it should've been."

"And Olive told me about the fight, but she told me she didn't know if it was true or not. And now I find out that it is, as well as it was Olivia that had gotten into the fight with Kat because Olive told me she didn't know who it was that Kat had gotten into a fight with if the fight rumor was true, now I find out that it was Olivia."

"She knew it was true, Kitty. She also knew it was Olivia, she just didn't wanna tell you. She just wanted to pretend to you that she didn't know for sure, that's all. But we left it out of the story because we just felt that the cops didn't have to know that. We just said we got into a verbal argument with Kat which was true, and that was it, and she was upset because we didn't want her to be in the group so she just got in her car and stormed off."

"Oh, wow," I said. "I mean, it doesn't seem like the fight was that big of a deal because she didn't die because of it. She died because she obviously made a wrong turn and accidentally went into the lake."

"But her head injury could've caused that to happen since she hit her head on the side rearview mirror of her car after Olivia punched her very hard in the face. We don't know, Kitty, and I think it's something that we will never know. Or it could've been the alcohol or drugs she was on because she was definitely drunk and high which everyone knows effects your judgement especially while driving, or a combination or all three, who knows? Plus, while her and Olivia were fighting, Kat's phone was knocked out of her hand by Olivia, so Kat drove off without even realizing it so if she was in trouble and went into that lake, she could've called 911 before being completely submerged in the water, but she didn't have her phone plus she had a head injury along with being drunk and high, and that made her completely helpless at that point."

"That's very true. So, one of you picked her phone up?" I asked, as I stared at her.

"Hey, it wasn't me," she informed me.

"Who did?"

"Whoever did has it to this day. I actually didn't see who it was because I was so busy cheering on Olivia while she was fighting Kat."

I started to get chills all over again. And just when I thought this case was over with. They actually lied to the cops about it because withholding information was the same as lying, and they confirmed this about the fight Olivia and Kat got into when we were all at Prima's house after all the charges were dropped against them. "You all withheld a very important piece of information about the case, and that was the fight. My goodness, how could all of you do that?"

"Like I said, it was something the cops didn't have to know, Kitty. We didn't know Kat was gonna run her car in the lake that night after that fight, and now you know what could've caused that to happen. It was one of the three things that I'd mentioned, or it could've been something else that none of us know about and will never know about. This still isn't our fault and I will stand by it. Now that you know the truth that you didn't get from the PGs, I really hope you don't say anything about it because there's nothing anyone can do for Kat."

"Actually, I did get the truth from them since they talked about this *after* the charges were dropped against them. And I think that was their way of feeling that they were coming clean about it because there was no proof that the fight caused Kat to make a wrong turn and go into the lake. But I know there isn't anything anyone can do for her, but there is something you all can do for her family."

"And what is that, Kitty?"

"Give them back her phone. Zoe was asking me about it, and it's clear that one of you have it. Even if you have to mail it back to them, I think they deserve to have it. They feel it's one of the only things they'll have back from that night, but Zoe told me she doesn't think they'll ever find it, but you just told me that one of the PGs has it. I think that's sick, Poppy."

"All of this is sick, Kitty, but it is what it is. But I don't think you're gonna think the Kat case is as sick as you think mine is."

A nervous wave of chills rippled through me once again. "What is going on with your case, Poppy? The PGs wanna know. They also wanna know why you're ignoring them now. They wanna know why you haven't been back to school. Are you coming back?"

"Not for the rest of this year. It's only a little over a month and a half left so I'm just gonna finish this year online. Principal Harden approved it for me to do since he knows what happened to me, well, everyone knows."

"Do you want me to let the PGs know you're not gonna be back for the rest of the year?"

She sighed. "No."

I shook my head. "I'm over here now talking to you, Poppy, face to face, something that you haven't done with them since your incident, and they're really pissed about it. They've been talking bad about you because of it, saying that you're not gonna be in the group anymore if you don't talk to them."

"Doesn't surprise me that they're saying these things, Kitty. They threatened Olivia that they were gonna kick her out of the group if she told the truth about what'd happened in Kat's case. I think their threats and everything is what really drove her to suicide. She wanted to tell the truth about there being a physical fight between her and Kat, not just a verbal one, because she felt that it led to Kat's demise because of her hitting her head on her side rearview mirror therefore effecting her judgement when she drove. We tried and tried to tell her it wasn't her fault and that anything could happen in a fight, but she felt so bad about it, and at least I couldn't blame her for that. We even went as far as trying to convince her that Kat could've blacked out from the drugs and alcohol that she had in her that night and ran off the road somewhere, but none of us ever thought it would be into the lake; it never even crossed our minds until we found out it actually happened. But she didn't know what to believe because there were so many possibilities. But she never got over it, obviously."

"Yeah, it's unfortunate that she never did. This has all been such a sad situation, and now I feel that you all weren't completely honest with the authorities about what'd happened, and in turn that made me dishonest because I only went on what you all told me."

"But you're not dishonest because you only went on what you were told, Kitty. But like I said, there's nothing we can do about it now, and I feel that my case is of importance just as much as Kat's. I'm not saying that Kat's never was, and I won't ever say that."

"But that's what we wanna do is help you, Poppy, but you're not letting us. Why are you ignoring all of the PGs except me, huh? They really wanna know."

"And what I really wanna know is were all of you together sitting in a circle in one of y'alls bedrooms with your phones on speakers taking turns calling me that one day when I got all of those calls from you all in a row?"

"Yes," I replied without hesitation with a slight grin. "How did you know?"

"I just know the PGs, Kitty, since I am one."

"But they're threatening to kick you out of the group because you won't talk to them or let them see you, Poppy, like the way I'm doing right now."

"I know. I've seen every post that PG blog does. I've seen and read every single one since they started it. If they only knew everything, Kitty."

"And it's like they think I know everything because they're always telling me to contact them, but I can't do that because Prima and the rest of them pretty much threatened me not to, so I really wanna adhere to what they say. If it wasn't for them, I wouldn't be a PG and have all of you as friends and all and have people like me and every-thing. I know things haven't been perfect, but at least I'm not a lonely person because as the new girl, I could've very well ended up like that."

"And trust me, Kitty, in a lot of ways you would've been better off."

I gasped. "Well, I think being around people and having friends is important, Poppy. I just didn't know that I would have this much drama this soon at my new school. I know drama is a part of life, but this even surprised me."

She smiled. "Yeah, I know it did. But I still feel that you should find new friends and try to get out now while you still can."

I sipped on my drink as I stared at her. "Why? There's a reason why you're saying this, Poppy. What's really going on between you and the PGs, huh? Why do you want me to leave them? Why won't you talk to them? You still haven't told me why?"

She continued to stare at me as if she wasn't gonna answer my millions of questions, but I was not gonna stop asking them.

"What, Poppy? What is it? Why are you acting like this towards them? They've done so much for you, you know, the vigil and all, and you're treating them like they're your enemies, they even said that."

"Yeah, funny how they would say that. The mind games, wow."

"What do you mean?"

She shook her head and refused to say a word. The look in her eyes had chilled me to the bone. It was clear she didn't wanna tell me about the mind games, and looked at me as if I should've known what she was talking about.

"Kitty, remember when you thought you were losing all of those calls while talking to me?"

"Yes, I remember."

"You didn't lose them. I hung up when I heard one of the PGs talking to you."

"Oh, my God, Poppy! But why?"

"Because I didn't want them to know you were talking to me."

"But *why?*"

She still held that look in her eyes and I was still so chilled to the bone I felt like I needed a coat now even though it was in the 90s out here.

"Kitty, all of their talk about caring for me isn't what it seems, okay? I think they're master manipulators, especially to you because they know they can say anything to you and you'll believe them. Like I said, they're playing mind games with you. Psychological shit at its finest."

"Well, I don't know about believing everything they say to me now," I admitted. "Poppy, you're really scaring me. Please tell me what's going on?"

She sighed. "Get out while you can, Kitty. I'm serious."

"Now you're *really scaring me,* Poppy. Please, *please* tell me who did this to you? You know who did this to you now, don't you? Your memory came back about that day, hasn't it?"

"Yes," she replied without hesitation.

"Oh, my God," I said. I took a very deep breath. "Who hurt you that day in the bathroom at school? You could've been killed and now you know who did it? *You know* you can tell me. Who did this to you?"

Her eyes narrowed on me and were as cold as they could be. "The PGs."

POPULAR GIRLS
ACCUSED
POPULAR GIRLS SERIES #2

PG Poppy has made an unbelievable accusation and no one knows whether or not to believe her, and she now has no idea just what's in store for her because of this accusation alone, while PG Kitty tries to figure out whose side she should be on, or should she leave everything and everyone while she still can.

ABOUT THE AUTHOR

Sheila Michelle is an author of young adult books. When she's not writing about influential girls in fancy clothes, she enjoys watching YouTube videos, Amazon Prime Video, and reading a variety of non-fiction books.